A MINOR CHORUS

A MINOR CHORUS

A NOVEL

BILLY-RAY BELCOURT

W. W. NORTON & COMPANY
Independent Publishers Since 1923

A Minor Chorus is a work of fiction. Names, characters, places, and incidents are the products of the author's imagination or are used fictitiously. Any resemblance to actual events, locales, or persons, living or dead, is entirely coincidental.

For information about permission to reproduce selections from this book, write to Permissions, W. W. Norton & Company, Inc., 500 Fifth Avenue, New York, NY 10110

For information about special discounts for bulk purchases, please contact W. W. Norton Special Sales at specialsales@wwnorton.com or 800-233-4830

Manufacturing by Lakeside Book Company
Book design by Beth Steidle
Production manager: Beth Steidle

ISBN 978-1-324-02142-1

W. W. Norton & Company, Inc., 500 Fifth Avenue, New York, N.Y. 10110
www.wwnorton.com

W. W. Norton & Company Ltd., 15 Carlisle Street, London W1D 3BS

1 2 3 4 5 6 7 8 9 0

For my kokum, who made
all my writing possible

A MINOR CHORUS

A guard handcuffs me and pushes me away from the visitors'
station. In my unit, there's a small room just off the foyer with
a glass ceiling. When it's sunny, I sit in there and think about
everything that's ever happened to me. When I woke up this
morning, I felt the heat before I opened my eyes and knew the
sky was blue. If I'm allowed, I think I'll stay in there for the
rest of the day. I'll close my eyes and end up somewhere else
for a little while. Maybe I'll end up back on the rez. Before
I learned to drive, I walked along a winding dirt road from
my house near the lake to the center of the rez where most of
my cousins lived. If I concentrate hard enough, if I drown out
the noise of the other inmates and the officers, I might hear
the rocks shift under my feet. I might hear the birds and the
barking dogs and the wind in the trees and someone's uncle
telling someone's kids to stay safe. And, if I can empty my

mind enough, forget where I am for a second or two, I might remember what it felt like when, upon returning, I'd see Kokum waiting for me on the patio as if she could sense that I was nearby. Even from far away, I would see her waving at me, smiling.

1

A PROBLEM OF FORM

It was a late afternoon at the start of August when I went to the university to meet up with River, a dear friend and graduate student in the Department of Sociology who hailed from a reserve to the south, to make sense of the desire to remake my life. I wanted to leave academia. This thought, which wasn't so much intrusive as it was a response to an ongoing crisis of creativity, permeated my days.

I was waiting in front of one of the oldest buildings on campus, a neoclassical hallmark of the humanities quad called

Old Arts. The entrance was replete with tributes to the architecture of antiquity; on either side of the steps were pillars and above each of those were an even larger pair. Foliage sprawled across the façade, illuminating rather than obscuring the ornate brickwork. Because it was outside the normal academic year, there was no one else around me. The effect of all of this was that in my Cree body in the twenty-first century I was a historical anomaly. On this day I was fine with projecting my feelings of alienation onto what was so clearly a product of a longing for a heroic white past, however mythological. In fact, it felt rebellious to do so.

It wasn't that I had been wronged by the university per se. Rather, something inside me shifted in the last year such that I was no longer moved to play by its rules. I was meant to be writing a dissertation, but what the sentences I'd been compiling in a document really added up to was a depression diary or a lover's discourse. I'd been writing about the politics of race and sadness, yes, but most days this "research topic" was more accurately a kind of self-directed behavioral therapy. I'd been experiencing life as a problem of form: it is difficult to live in a world that corrodes freedom. The shape of my days was fuzzy, imprecise. My body took on that fuzziness. I wanted to take a sledgehammer to the past to let in the shimmer of a light I didn't know was there all along. It seemed unavoidable that I now wanted my writing not to advance an institutional body of knowledge, as is the case with a dissertation, but instead to invent an exit route, to make something out of nothing, to prop up a landmark for a place that was nowhere and everywhere. At first I assumed that because I felt both uprooted and stuck I was going through a more acute depressive episode than usual, but I realized that I had been overtaken by new ambitions, a more consuming kind of hunger—a hunger for another way of being in the world. I couldn't unsee everything my gut told me I was missing out on.

It was still summer nonetheless and there was still the greenery, which was so lush and overwhelming it was something of an argument for optimism, a reminder that I had to be alert to the beauty in excess, the beauty in things that quietly endured despite their unbeautiful contexts. If I admired my own abundances, my own little rebellions against subjugation, I reasoned, I could learn to be as alive as possible. It seemed silly I hadn't come to this conclusion sooner.

As always, River looked effortlessly queer. Their dress was structured unconventionally, defying geometrical norm, and because of this it told a story of an interesting inner world. I smiled at the sight of it. We were seated at a table near the back wall. The café was a campus staple and was typically at capacity from September through April, emptier now given the student exodus from the neighborhood over summer. The mood was artful, liberal—a Phoebe Bridgers song was playing overhead. The most memorable aspect of the establishment was its walls, which over the years had been graffitied by patrons and commissioned artists from around the world. Above my head, for example, was a drawing of a police car that had been set ablaze. And beside River was an almost invisible sentence that sounded to us like the rallying cry of our generation: "Write poems, eat ass, & dismantle private property." They took a picture of the quote to post to Instagram later.

River studied arts-based anti-oppressive education. Their research project was community-driven: they worked with inner city organizations to administer programs aimed at Indigenous youth empowerment. We'd met during our coursework year in a class called Politics & Gender. It was a small seminar with a professor who became popular and beloved for never assigning texts authored by men. Our bond was citational (we read the same scholars) as well as circumstantial (we were the only Indigenous students in the course and resultantly gravitated toward each other). Soon after, it became familial: we studied together in the library, roomed together at conferences, went on annual "gaycations" to the west coast. Our friendship felt metaphysically ordained. Alas, time had gotten away from us; it'd been weeks since we'd last seen each other.

How's fieldwork been? I asked. From what I've seen online, you've been incredibly busy.

Fieldwork's been magical, River said. The other day I did a writing workshop using Audre Lorde's poems on silence and her calls to build alternative models of social action that uplift the oppressed. The youth really got it, wrote these heartbreaking poems about what they wished they could say if they could figure out how to not be afraid. At the end of the session, I told them they did figure it out, that they weren't as afraid as they thought they were. I cried.

So it is better to speak remembering we were never meant to survive. "A Litany for Survival," right? I said.

Exactly. I teach it whenever I get the chance.

I wrote that line on the mirror in my bedroom in my first-ever apartment, I said. It's such an egalitarian notion. I felt caressed by it. I felt that Lorde gave me access to an openness I hadn't had before. By virtue of what we as marginalized peoples have survived, against the odds, we speak with at minimum a kind of political possibility. Our ancestors very literally survived genocide. I don't think I'll ever be able to process the magnitude of that. One of the most enduring problems of my twenties, I continued, is that few, especially those in power, allow that knowledge to alter how they act. That's a kind of silence we have to live with, isn't it?

Yes, yes, it's absorbing, River said. That makes me think of how for years now we've been protesting injustice after injustice and as a result our way of being in the world is always shifting. In the midst of tragedy, we wake up differently and go to bed differently. Then I walk through campus and it feels as if nothing of concern is happening elsewhere.

Remember when that professor told me that I was lucky to be able to write from lived experience, that that made me more valuable on the job market these days? I asked. He said it with such nonchalance and exactitude. I walked away. I didn't want to cause a commotion, but I wish I would've said, *Do you know what you're saying to me? That my suffering is an economic privilege?* What a brutal worldview, I said to River, that everything has a kind of exploitable value, regardless of its personal toll.

That kind of misknowing is everywhere, River said. My research, my work, I suppose, aims to combat that.

I think my problem is that I don't know what social good my research has, I said. I spend all this time alone in my apartment writing about the grief of being queer and Cree in a settler state while that grief compounds. I haven't even been writing lately; I've been binge-watching all sixteen seasons of *Grey's Anatomy*. I stayed up late for weeks. I got so dehydrated I had to see a doctor. I literally gave myself hemorrhoids.

We laughed at how tweetable my despair was.

Oh dear, River said. Not *Grey's Anatomy*. All right, things are, let's say, serious. What's your heart telling you?

It's telling me that I should quit.

I felt too much emotion to say anything else. River reached for my hand.

When did this all start? I know it might be impossible to know, they said.

It's been a pestering thought for a while now. I've given up so much to be a student; I've been in school for all my adult life. I've forgone dating and hobbies and artistic growth to read post-structural theory. So now I'm, like, maybe Foucault was wrong, maybe I'm not as free as I think I am. So many grad students are so fucking miserable—maybe the whole thing is rotten.

I hear you, River said, but for what it's worth I think I'm an example of a more pragmatic approach to grad school. I've secured enough funding to pay my bills, made sure I had a committee with mostly Indigenous scholars, jumped through all the hoops as strategically and as quickly as possible. I'm planning to defend my dissertation this time next year. Then I'll move on. I'll go back to the rez.

River intends to take over the Education Department on their rez, but they especially want to implement programming that does the work of consciousness-raising so that youth don't have to leave their rez to learn about politics and history, as was the case with us. They intend to be a queer presence in the community, to open up space to talk about and revitalize culturally specific notions of sexuality and gender. They have a theory that reserves are fundamentally rebellious spaces by virtue of band members making joy in the face of carceral power. Why couldn't they also be shelters for queer and trans Indigenous life? All their community needed, they hypothesized, was the infrastructure, the right people, an ethos of social change.

Graduate school for me is a means to an end, they added.

I guess I wanted too much, I said. I fell in love with ideas as an undergrad. I wanted to write like every queer theorist I read.

That makes complete sense, River said dryly.

I laughed. The lushness of their prose felt to me like an extension of their sexual identities. With beautiful ideas, they could reclaim their bodies from the history of language as a collective weapon.

No job seemed more perfect for me than a professor, I continued. But then I took a required seminar on professionalization and realized I may not even get hired. Who knows how long universities will be interested in recruiting Indigenous scholars? Reconciliation's dying. The government said sorry and now everyone's moving on. They'll stop hiring us in the name of austerity. I paused. The political standard I hold myself to, I said, is that I have to exist in the world so as to refuse it. Graduate school is hardly the place to end white supremacist heteropatriarchal capitalism.

We both sighed. The problem: universities are institutions inside which one could feel as if they were doing radical work when in actuality that radical work was being coopted and diminished and transformed into "diversity" and "equity" data. Despite our idealism, despite our elegantly articulated methodologies of resistance, our research output would likely be called forth as evidence of a structural reckoning that wasn't happening, not in any substantial sense. Universities weren't in the business of giving the land back, for example.

It does suck, River said. I have—we have—seen amazing, badass thinkers and activists pushed out or deradicalized by the university. It's like what Fred Moten said: As racialized people we can only really be in a relation of criminality to the university. We have to steal from it. In my case, I'm rerouting resources to youth, back to my rez.

Sometimes I think I have to steal myself away, I said.

What would you do instead?

I hesitated. I still want to write, I said. I've been trained to see the novel as this capacious and possibly dissident form for the articulation of social life. I've been thinking: What if I wrote one myself? I'd reach a larger audience. I could represent the lives of queer and Cree people without the constraints of scholarly norms. I could write a book about northern Alberta. There's so much to be said about what it is to be in a place that history has so thoroughly shaped. My writing is so embodied, so full of longing, I tend toward the poetic all the time, there's

a kind of music I'm trying to generate, I think. What if I've
been working in the wrong mode this entire time?

I was ad-libbing, but I was abuzz with the euphoria
of something that felt like political transformation. I was
like a character in a Virginia Woolf novel: *There must be
another life.*

I'd read the fuck out of that novel, River said. As always,
their compassion buoyed me. But, with an air of concern, they
added, Have you ever written fiction?

I read novels all the time, I said, but also I don't think
theory and prose, or whatever you want to call it, are that
distant. They both ask us to refuse a romance of the present.
They're streets in the same city, and sometimes they intersect.
I think I'm already planted at that intersection. I'm already
under its streetlights.

I think you should trust this impulse, go into it, go deeper
into the joyfulness, River said. It was an expression of their
personhood to advocate on behalf of another's freedom. In
their company, I felt less lonely. I was squarely inside something like pure possibility, a feeling I hadn't felt in what seemed
like ages. I didn't want to say anything that would rupture the
clarity and spaciousness of River's sentimentality.

You're such an angel. I want to be like you when I grow
up, I said finally, even though we were the same age. River
seemed to have access to a wisdom I'd only ever stumble onto.

They had to get to an evening shift at a downtown shel-
ter, so we parted ways. Let me know how everything unfolds!
Remember: the Creator is on your side! They yelled as they
rode away on a bike.

Love you, I said, though it was stifled by the sounds of passing cars.

I was stuck in morning traffic the next day on the High Level Bridge, suspended above the North Saskatchewan River, the ancient waterway Indigenous peoples traversed for centuries. Today, though, too-large vehicles were moving slowly in both directions, clogged in one of the few bridges that connected the north and south sides of the city. Here was just one example, I thought, of the many agonies of living in colonial times.

I had slept too long to catch the train, but I was now going to be late nonetheless. The stuckness felt like an analogy for my stint as a doctoral student. I was near the end of my third year in the program and had produced only about ninety double-spaced pages of misshapen paragraphs and fragments that included sentences like, *The body riots and I'm inside it, bearing witness, interpreting, translating, emoting,* and *The body is a myth or a ghost or a horror story or a beast of burden, depends on who you ask.* Some of them were scattered in various notebooks like forgotten memories. What my supervisor had read, she admired. She said I was reinventing the genre of the dissertation, seeing what it could and couldn't contain. I wanted to believe her, but I also had questions about the social life of writing that I couldn't find an answer to because I was alone most of the time. There had been days when anything looked like a counter to being a graduate student: news of a flower blooming once every twelve years, a man's pulsating body beside mine. Today, even: the sunlight pirouetting around me. The difference was that right now my hope was neither hypothetical nor temporary. I was going to make something that was the opposite of a country: beautiful.

My supervisor's office had a wall of windows, through which I could see the entirety of a golf course that snaked through the river valley. Her name was Hannah and she was a scholar who specialized in the study of anti-oppressive poetics. She didn't teach Indigenous literature, but I'd taken her class on the history of grassroots, community-based literary cultures as an undergrad and I felt a kind of affective bond grounded in intellectual awe. She was the smartest person I knew. Although she held all the institutional privileges that came with tenure, she still exhibited a subtle anti-institutional bent and fostered it in her students. She was, it should be said, nonetheless of the mind that if you managed to be in the university with the right credentials you could do good work; you could, as Gayatri Spivak put it, non-coercively inspire students to rearrange their desires away from neoliberal learning outcomes (the student as consumer, knowledge as commodity) and toward freedom, however partial and incomplete. What I was about to discuss with her was, it could be argued, a symptom of her pedagogical habits. That I wanted to eschew academic study for another kind, one less regimented and more communal, wouldn't be much of a surprise, I hoped.

When I arrived at her office door she heard my footsteps and said, Please, come in. She was seated in a chair between a computer desk overflowing with what I assumed to be graduate student essays and a stylish mid-century modern couch over which was draped a Pendleton blanket. She was dressed fashionably, in a collared dress and vintage high tops, a curious contrast that said, *Juxtaposition is an aesthetic miracle*, or at least that's what I read into it. Against one wall was a massive bookshelf inside which the history of critical theory unraveled, from the "Nothing isn't an expression of power" folks to the "A body is an archive of all the world's beauty and terror" folks to the newer, more poetic "The future is already here, we just have to claim it" folks. Where I stood on the spectrum could change from one hour to the next. Usually I felt everything all the time.

Hannah exuded warmth, which made me feel braver than I was.

Okay, wow, I'm nervous, I said to Hannah, who furrowed her brow in concern and leaned forward. I want to talk to you about my dissertation. The thing is, I can't write it, I confessed.

Hannah looked compassionately at me, as she had done many times before, a compassion that seemed to acknowledge that we were situated inside a structure that depleted more than it enlivened.

Is it that you're stuck because of methodological or analytical reasons? she asked. Do you want to discuss strategies for productivity? You know I'm happy to think with you about your ideas, to be an interlocutor. I can look back at your previous excerpt. I remember finding it very moving. She said all this quickly; it struck me that she might be feeling at least somewhat to blame, especially given the unloading of care and emotional labor to individuals, particularly women and people of color, that characterizes academia.

It's nothing you haven't done, I clarified. If anything, I'm indebted to you in a way I could never repay. The truth is that for a while now I've been weighing the decision to stay or to leave the program. I'm two years away from a defense; the thought of remaining a student with funding that is barely livable and a life that seems like a worse version of Barthes's "solitude with regular interruptions"—because the regular interruptions have been racism and bureaucratic violence—is unbearable. And I don't want to bear the unbearable. Sometimes I gaslight myself because from afar I'm doing something that syncs up with my intellectual goals. Despite getting glimpses of the unlivability of the institution in my MA, I still started the Ph.D. with a lofty dream: to produce an academic work of cultural significance. Now I'm not sure that's what I want anymore, nor do I believe that's even possible.

Throughout all of this Hannah nodded, solemn. At one point she shook her head supportively. I was certain she had heard a version of this story before, if not gone through it herself. I often marveled at her ability to weather the difficulties of the neoliberalizing machine we had put our bodies inside of. She was an expert in seeming complacent while building a cooperative of rebellion in her seminar rooms. There, we could be more than data; we could, without shame, think up the contours of another university, another world. I remember, for example, one session in which Hannah led us into the river valley to write little poems for and with the trees in the style of Yoko Ono's *Grapefruit*. The point was to make use of a writing practice that was in concert with the earth, that wasn't about the singular "I" we'd been elsewhere instructed to pledge allegiance to the way one does a nation. She was teaching us to be citizens of the air and water and sunlight. Afterward, I felt that I inhabited my body differently, and that this was the kind of pedagogy and intellectual culture I ached for, but later I was once more engulfed by sadness at the realization I hadn't encountered it until that moment. This experience, it turned out, would be devastatingly rare.

I hear everything you're saying, Hannah said, I really do. It's an existential problem. Doubt invades everything. I would kick myself, though, if I didn't remind you that your work is important and that you're doing something powerful, you're doing autotheory and it's non-traditional and we need it. But I also know that there are few to no methodologies that can cure loneliness or whatever you want to call what it feels like to be besieged by structural forces that assail our joy.

The other day, I said, I ended up at an anti-pipeline protest at the Legislature and the whole time I kept thinking, what if I wrote something that sounded like dozens of people in protest? These Cree women were chanting, "LAND BACK," into a microphone with an urgency older than the city, and it made me hope I could write in a way that didn't hold the country as an anthropological given. Is that even possible? Maybe what repels me about the dissertation is that it's so individualistic. Something I began thinking about in your class is that writing is fundamentally a social act. I write because I've read and been moved into a position of wonder. I write because I've loved and been loved. I want to find out what "we" or "us" I can walk into or build a roof over. To hold hands with others, really. To be less alone.

Listen, this is the kind of writing you can do here, with me, Hannah said. I can help you theorize your way out of the usual disciplinary conventions and strictures. Others have done semi-creative work in the past, though few, admittedly. Perhaps I could've communicated this better.

Hannah's emotionality emboldened me rather than spurred any second thoughts or regret. It was proof that I owed it to myself to at least pause to reflect on what I would have to forfeit to pursue an academic career. I also wondered if her willingness to commit to delicately balancing subversion and concession day in and out revealed a generational rift that meant we weren't looking through the same lens. She was of the perspective that one could occupy the center and bring the margin into its folds, to remake from within. But that had always seemed like an incitement for disaster to me. I had been born into a so-called margin; to me and my kin it was always-already the center, one among many.

Still, I struggled to pinpoint what exactly I wanted because what I wanted didn't always seem logical. I felt that errant wanting in my chest. My anxieties weren't just about writing but living; the two had become enmeshed.

I think I have to at least take a break. A month, perhaps. Experiment with other forms, trust my instincts. Maybe I'll go home, go north. God, it feels as though I've spent so little time there lately. Maybe I'll pretend that I'm not a doctoral student for a little while. Is that okay?

Of course it's okay, Hannah said. You have to protect

your art, nourish yourself. I'll be here, as always. Time isn't running out. There'll always be time. Hannah gave a smile that suggested she knew she could only say so much on behalf of an institution she herself was skeptical of. Whatever you do, she added, please take care of yourself.

As I left the English Department, I felt that I wasn't the same person, that I was at the beginning of a series of minor but purposeful reinventions. I was going to don a new "I" like shiny armor. Maybe because I was a hopeless romantic, maybe because I was prone to melodrama, this "I" seemed less despairing, more lyrical.

2

A GUST OF LIFE

On dating apps, I sometimes asked men to describe the texture of their grief. If I wasn't immediately blocked, most spouted platitudes or said something like, *Are you looking or not?* Those who did make it to my door were brief, nameless, untalkative. Usually they wanted me to be a room they could govern the limits of, paint a new shade of blue: hungry topaz, hungry sapphire. I'd developed the habit of hooking up with men after long evenings of working on my dissertation, of writing into the void, hurling myself at myself. For a while, this felt like an extension of my work, mostly because my sadness and horniness had become inextricably entangled. Perhaps unsurprisingly, neither what I wrote nor whom I met at all hours of the night made me feel much else other than dim and indistinct. What I wanted from sex I wanted from writing: to be more fully inside my body without encumbrance, to experience embodiment as something other than a catch-22. My body felt so thoroughly overdetermined by forces outside of me, yet it was the source of my livability, it literally coursed with life even as life was something I was being deprived of. Love, art, these were small portals, they allowed for transcendence. Maybe there was a kind of danger in how ravenous I was for that which placed me beside the present. It was too late in the day to fully pursue this epiphany to its logical end, especially after the conversation with Hannah that afternoon, so I opened Grindr.

I ended up messaging with a therapist. He'd heard of me, seen me around campus, which terrified me, ruptured the allure of anonymity. I was less interested in having sex with him and more interested in his knowledge, which I suppose is also a kind of eroticism. He asked me to send another photo to be sure I was who I said I was. I sent him a candid photo River had taken one afternoon at a campground about an hour east of the city. In it, you could see the tattoos on my knuckles, which spelled out my username: CREE HOMO. In my early twenty-something mind, the act was an homage to Barthes's famous declaration that language is a kind of skin. I interpreted the aphorism literally, wanted to turn my body into a book of sad poems. I convinced myself that the tattoo would amount to a small refusal of the ways colonial systems demanded my invisibility. I hadn't yet understood that visibility begot its own kind of endangerment.

He told me that the tattoo was sexy, that I was handsome, and sometimes that was all it took to win me over. So when he asked if he could come over I said yes. On my couch, surrounded by wobbly towers of books about loneliness and state-sanctioned oppression, we talked for an hour about how I thought the body was a human invention, a ruse, a story that's easy to digest. I told him about how it had been easy to pretend the sounds of the brutal earth weren't mounting to a crescendo around me. I didn't care if my woundedness was unsexy. All of this was ugly work. Surprisingly he wasn't turned off by my honesty; in fact, it aroused him, made him feel like he was someone I could empty onto. He experienced it as an intensity, a gravity pulling at him. It was late and I was lonely and I was in rehearsal for another kind of life, so I drew the blinds and unbuttoned his jeans. It was all over in thirty minutes.

Before he left, I told him that I was going to write a book about suffering and love and lovelessness; he was moved by the description, however vacuous it actually was. I asked what he thought I should include, and he said, "Forgetting who you are." At first I thought he meant something like dissociative amnesia, a psychological response to trauma that causes someone to literally forget significant things that once formed the basis of their identity. I decided instead he meant something like the act of hanging oneself up to dry forever. He was speaking for those who felt water-damaged by the world. He was speaking directly to me.

After he left, when I was alone in a throbbing silence, I thought, Maybe I'm predisposed to being a writer because I radiate emotion so openly. What if I'm a beautiful wound people dance inside of? Even though I knew they'd be asleep, I texted River: *sometimes when I have sex it feels like I'm a photograph a man takes off the wall and puts back somewhere else and for the rest of the night I feel a little crooked lmao.*

The next morning, I woke to a response from River: *it's hard not to marvel at how poetic you are about your anguish. but maybe that's the queer condition amirite??*

After two cups of coffee, I'd only written a couple sentences about the time I was denied care in an emergency room. The on-call doctor accused me of lying about the pain I was experiencing and then I was removed by two security guards, presumably because of the semantic disaster of being an Indigenous man in distress in the middle of the night. It was six a.m. and I had, against better judgment, driven myself to the hospital during what I would later find out was a gallstones attack. I thought I was dying. I returned home to suffer without an audience. I couldn't sit or stand still or lie down. I fell asleep in the bathtub, woke up in cold water hours later. "Rusty" was the only word I had for the effect of having a body with wounds that aren't recognized as wounds. Whether or not I could write my way back into an embodied space where repair was possible was a question I tasked myself with answering.

My days after the meeting with Hannah were blurry, shapeless. Mostly I sat in a café in a middle-class neighborhood and watched strangers eye me suspiciously or ignore me entirely. Tomorrow is a new day, the barista said. Tomorrow is a philosophical conundrum, I said to myself after he'd walked away.

I was in the world, restless. The world was around me, cacophonous, fluttering. Everything I wrote seemed comparatively noiseless, unalive. I had simply continued in the disaffected mode that characterized most of my time as a grad student. This disheartened me.

I decided to reread James Baldwin's *Giovanni's Room* to try to relive the awe I felt when I first read it; I'd written for hours after putting the book down. This time I was struck anew by Giovanni's assertion that homesickness is captivating only insofar as "home" is out of reach. The distance allows it to be imbued with inflated nostalgia. To return is to risk watching it explode. To write a novel about what one might lose, I supposed, was to live inside the sphere of nostalgia, to become a living monument, which, in the end, is a kind of poetic misfortune.

The only place I had ever left was northern Alberta. In the metaphysical darkness of my thinking and reading and writing I began to miss it.

I was a boy not long ago. I did as boys did, which means I climbed a tree on a weekday evening in search of a new fable.

Which means I ran through the boreal forest openmouthed in search of the edge of the world. I was so small I could be drowned out by the most unimposing gusts of wind.

On November 15, 1977, Barthes wrote this in his *Mourning Diary*: "I am either lacerated or ill at ease / and occasionally subject to gusts of life." My hypothesis on the morning of August 6 was this: a novel is a gust of life from another world.

August 6, midnight. I tossed my body at a stranger as if he were a gust of life.

August 7, dawn. Googled: reasons to live. Approximately nine billion results. Googled: how to write a novel. Eight hundred million results. That was almost a trillion arguments against death.

"Who am I? I'm just a writer. I write things down," wrote poet Richard Siken.

I'm a writer. I experiment with language and therefore with the unknown world. I'm a writer; I'm unoriginal in my suffering! Join me in the crowded streets of dull possibility!

The next morning I thought of the popular Mary Oliver lines: "Tell me, what is it you plan to do / with your one wild and precious life?" — *The Summer Day* !!!! — *

Become a novelist seemed a modest if not underwhelming and irresponsible answer. But what if the act of writing a novel, I wondered, enabled one to practice a way of life that negated the brutalities of race, gender, hetero- and homonor-

* Doesn't everything die at last, and too soon?

mativity, capital and property? Rather than change the world, a novel could index a longing for something else, for a different arrangement of bodies, feelings, and environments, one in which human flourishing wasn't inhibited for the marginalized, which seemed as urgent an act of rebellion as any.

A novel is a body of water from which I frantically wanted to drink. What would a novel attuned to rising sea levels and melting Arctic ice sheets look like? What would its structure be? I wondered. Would the words grow paler and paler as the story progressed? Until what was left was a stick figure or sentence drowning in the corner of a blank page? Was I up to the challenge of envisaging an ecological literature against premature civilizational collapse? Not now, not here.

I began to compile a list of provocative things contemporary writers said about the novel:

Arundhati Roy: A novel can be as complex as a city, with lanes and by-lanes.

Rachel Cusk: The moral problem of the novel is the presumption one can inhabit another's consciousness.

Édouard Louis: "I think a novel should be bold enough to attempt to define its own construction in a new way."

Alexander Chee: "The novel is already at the door. Waiting, but just for a little. It is the lover again, impatient again. Wanting again for you to know everything."

My own anxieties about the novel had to do with my hunch that English is much too compromised a language to engender a portrait of Indigenous life that isn't subsumed by colonial fantasies of our disrepair. Little in my arsenal seemed spacious enough to combat a centuries-old reading practice that made Indigenous peoples out to be bombs. How instead to make a novel into a bomb? How to plant a novel in the moral infrastructure of a corrupt nation? How to write sentences that go *tick, tick, tick*?

A novelist espoused on Twitter recently the popular adage that one has to write what one doesn't know, what one doesn't want to know. It sounded mysterious, disturbingly so. I had wanted to protest, without knowing why, but then figured that the aphorism had to do with the mechanics of the sentence, how words come together almost magically, improvisationally. This I firmly believed. I decided that if I were a word it would be "grieve," and it would be sprawled across my forehead, as both a demand and a self-description.

Why write a novel? There were the requisite answers: to think through questions that agitated thinkability—what is truth, what makes a livable life, who suffers and who injures, what is it to be in a world one didn't choose, et cetera. On the contrary, the news coming out of North America as of late was, in a sense, an ongoing refutation of the novel, of anything that wasn't direct action, that didn't have to do with an immediate insurgency against those whose disregard for the livability of the oppressed amounted to a politics of socially engineered mass death. A novel, then, could be an indictment of the novelist, evidence of his inaction, his carelessness.

A summer ago, a man was lying on my couch, shirtless. Our semen was caught in his black chest hair. I pushed my hand into the muck, smearing the proof of our non-singularity around. A midday light was like an all-consuming song, louder than we knew how to be. This belongs to the category of the novelistic, as so little of living does, I thought at the time. I swatted away the light the way one would a fly. He chuckled. I chuckled too, not because I was amused, but because I was still experimenting with how to be human.

The summer before, I was on an impromptu date with an older white man in his forties from Grindr. I was twenty, entering the third year of an undergraduate degree. At a restaurant, we bonded over having both come to the city from rural places where there were few-to-no visible queers. At the end of the date, I went back to his place, a downtown condo with an unobstructed view of the river. Around us were eight-by-ten paintings and photographs by local Edmonton artists. I was impressed by the stainless-steel appliances, by the towering bookshelf, by the IKEA lamp that hung over the living room like a cloud, all of which represented a social legibility he fashioned over years and my youthful yearning for quick access to it. After making small talk, we kissed with an intensity I brought to almost all my sexual encounters—I was still so new to sex that a raw, primal ecstasy whirled inside me every time, like someone winding the hands of a wall clock forward after hours of disuse. I bore heavily into him, as if the skin were no longer a border but the positive absence of one and our two bodies could become a single entity, as if this act of recombination were the rightful state of embodiment for all animals of our disposition. Suddenly, he tossed me against a wall (playfully), then pushed my face into it (menacingly), narrowly missing a black-and-white bird's-eye view of the

Legislature. This is what you want, isn't it? he said, his voice denser than I had heard it all night, citing, for the first time, a history of cruel speech. Pressure built up in my skull, but it wasn't akin to a headache. It felt like my head was going to concave or crumple, like a water bottle or a sheet of paper. For ten seconds I was already dead, then readied myself to die or to suffer gracefully, which is the captive's last survival tactic. I shut my eyes. I was the antihero of this tragedy. I felt as if he had reached through my chest and squeezed my heart. Miraculously, I squirmed out of his hold, then ran all the way home, for twenty minutes, not breathing or breathing one long breath—I couldn't tell which was which. I ran ahead of my body, into bodilessness, without shoes on. Since then, I had always thought that if I were to write a book I would write this down. So, here, have it.

Some days my will to write a novel outweighed my will to live. That I can distinguish between the two is a coping mechanism.

In the end, the idea came to me suddenly, as I was walking with River in a park near their neighborhood. We were talking about the summer night I had sex with a man in the basement of a parking garage. I said it was the most alive I had ever been because I felt so close to death. "Don't worry, I'm not going to kill you," the man said before he stripped naked. River said people didn't naturally make the kinds of decisions I did when I was cruising. Once we stopped laughing, it occurred to me that I wanted to examine how we live under conditions of duress, both visible and invisible. My novel, then, would be a kind of literary ethnography of sadness and hope, of constraint and possibility. My informants would all come from the same place: the town in which I was raised, in a region heretofore unexplored in Canadian letters. I would write a book that reflected a community's emotional lives rather than just my sensory experience of the present. I would drive into town with graffitied fists and make art that would matter. If I wanted to study what was and wasn't worth living for, I told River, I had to make the trek to northern Alberta. They bought us a second round of coffees as a celebratory gesture.

Within hours, I had devised a methodology: I would collect the testimonies of those who were, in an existential sense, contortionists, people whose personal histories were marked by structural neglect, by cruel fate, by heavy silence, by a joy that pressurized sociological theories of deficiency. Why not do this in Edmonton? For starters, it represented a past life I disavowed, it stood for an embargo on creativity and revolution. It was true that anywhere history could fabricate a world, could become the contours of a body, a person, a house, a neighborhood; I suspected, however, that in some places and not others this fact was hidden. There was nothing new to say about the city, and everything still to say about the outskirts of the modern, about the zones of existence where the present was always the past, or, more precisely, was always the past reverberating like the aftershocks of an earthquake. Rural Alberta was where I'd reacquaint myself with the preciousness and wildness of life. In talking to those who came from where

I came from, I also hoped light would be shed on the person I was or the person I might become. Perhaps I was no longer repressing the fact that I was as determined as anyone else by the milieu into which I was born.

This is what I know about where I come from: it's a place where history begins and ends. Before it was part of Alberta, it was the District of Athabasca, and before that it didn't have an English name. It's the homeland of the Cree and Dene and Métis, and for centuries my ancestors lived in harmony with the land and water and forests and animals. At the close of one century and the start of another, those from whom I descend signed a treaty near the shores of the lake around which many reserves are now located, including my own. They signed in the spirit of communality and peace and in the name of future generations, though what followed was an era defined by a systematic assault on Indigenous livability: death schools, open-air prisons, child abductions. Many sick experiments were carried out by the federal government and its hench-men from which we're still recovering; though recovery isn't always an option. All the while people resisted, loudly and quietly, but always creatively. This was one way to tell a story about northern Alberta. There was another way, one that was embodied and consequential for the living, one that zoomed in on emotion and intimacy. It was this more corporeal mode of storytelling that enticed me.

What I knew about being queer and Indigenous and in my twenties was desperation. It is we who experience alive-ness as both inescapable and a shimmering impossibility. We improvise life outside the frame of futurity while also being ensnared by it. We don't die. We proliferate life as if machines engineered to do so; that's it. I would return to my hometown and go about the practice of not dying, I thought. My liveliness would be artful.

Death itself wasn't nearly as devastating as what the human drive to stay alive causes us to accumulate over time. We endure with quaking certainty; the world devastates us without end and still we are hungry and hungrier. What dazzling logic.

In a matter of days, I confirmed a number of interviewees, all of whom were amiable and eager to participate, a symptom, to my mind, of an urge to perform the novelistic as a kind of abstract moral value (an urge I found relatable). During the phone calls, it occurred to me that so few of us are given permission to theorize about our lives, so many are bound to the register of everyday chitchat. It made me wonder: If there isn't time or space to account for or to avow with bewilderment and frustration and joy the emotional fabric of one's life, to assert one's enmeshment in a narrative of humanness that continues to unfold, where does that language go, where does it pile up? Inside us, as routinized as oxygen? Or is it like dust, a porous, vulnerable, almost unperceivable film covering everything? In one's mouth, would it taste like the earth?

Once I'd made arrangements and packed my vehicle with my bags, with books I treated like talismans, I drove northward out of the city and, in so doing, deeper into my homeland. I drove for four hours through central Alberta and into the boreal forest, along the southern edge of the subarctic. I whirled past rows and rows of trees, which, blurred by speed, looked like a wall I could knock over. Upon crossing the Athabasca River, I pulled over in front of a sign that marked the division between Treaty 6 and Treaty 8, an old but not ancient division I felt called to acknowledge. After a few minutes I darted away, shoving my palms into the off-white bark of a single poplar. I swear, for a second or two the whole forest shook.

As I made my way from one side of the province's third largest lake to the other, I passed through reserves as well as predominantly white villages and hamlets, one after the other, a pattern that could only have been devised from of a colonizer's militaristic imagination, and maybe it was. There were swaths of forest around the reserves and farmers' fields in between, especially so around my hometown. Nothing was inextricable from the trauma of the twentieth century, everything was bound up in colonial policy, in the processes of racialization and settlement, yet the topography was gorgeous, yet my people were still so full of life. I was a product of this paradox, and I had returned to study it.

3

A FAMILIAR FACE

I was seated at a bench in what wasn't so much a park but a rough draft of one, surrounded by four transplanted spruce trees in the shape of a square. Blades of grass rebelliously sprung through the cobblestone underfoot. I could see my hotel in the distance. I told my family I'd chosen to stay there so as not to disturb whatever summer plans had been set in motion months ago, an explanation they were happy to accept as an act of generosity, as few were home anyway. From here, the hotel, located in a pseudo-industrial district (mostly consisting of car dealerships and automotive shops), appeared to sprout from miles and miles of canola, which imbued the building with a poetic charm I presumed was an architectural accident, something I read too much into, unless of course one could derive a kind of poetry from either coincidence or the likelihood that such a sight repeated in mid-sized towns throughout the prairies. A poetic image, after all, can be a mistake that, through repetition, through luck, acquires the ability to say, *So what?* not out of laziness or disaffection but in defiance to the sovereignty of the "I," a reiteration of how art exceeds individual consciousness. Maybe this was why I wanted to write a novel: to be reminded that not even my puny life with its puny preoccupations and miseries was mine alone to shoulder. I want to be reckless, which is to say unsentimental, with my suffering. So often the creative impulse is an impulse to build something that, in the end, its maker can't destroy, something that outgrows intention. Isn't a town also indestructible in this sense? Don't we submit to it, doesn't it already sculpt us, before we even begin to think it was we who built it, we who dug our hands into the clay of the ordinary and made something permanent and irrepressible?

Around me stood buildings and storefronts, most of them built in the previous century, housing either recently closed businesses or ones that struggled to stay open. I couldn't imagine anything but transnational chains making a substantial profit around here anymore. So many from the area, including relatives, had resorted to taking up jobs in the oil fields once the mills could no longer function as the area's primary economic engine. Now the resource extraction industry was something of a last hope for many northern Albertans. This fact made me want to write another book about how under capitalism to live and work is to be against the population of which you're a part.

Directly across from me was a long-unoccupied building believed to have been constructed in the early days of colonial encroachment in this part of the province. It was a safety hazard, falling apart, caving in on itself. The farther one veered from Main Street, a single stretch of highway on which sat most of the town's businesses, schools, and amenities, the older the infrastructure became. Behind the dilapidating building ran train tracks that were less like sutures and more like wounds. It all looked so ordinary and Canadian and, because of this, haunted.

When I'd arrived at the hotel the night before, I ordered room service and listened to one of the region's radio stations before bed. I heard a story about a group of Indigenous midwives mobilizing to revive cultural birthing practices. The representative spoke about the country's history of forced sterilization, the looming threat of social services at present-day hospitals, and the many ancestral teachings about motherhood they were hoping to better popularize. I was inspired by the segment and it seemed like a good omen, a sign I likewise could breach the sound barriers of historical ignorance that surround rural Alberta.

I stood up as a mud-splattered maroon van pulled up to the sidewalk a few meters away; out of its passenger door climbed Mary, an elderly woman from a neighboring reserve who was my great-aunt. Atop her cheekbones, below her eyebrows, were crow's feet, slightly inverted dashes, as if her eyes indicated a break from a regular thought, a jolt. Under a fleece zip-up, she was wearing an orange shirt on which stick figures held hands in a circle around her torso to memorialize survivors of the Indian residential school system. She gripped my right hand with both of hers. Zap.

My boy, she exclaimed, a term of endearment that to my ear had at least partly to do with a disinterest in the nuclear family as the sealed container for affection and care (a Western export). I'm so happy to see you—look at you! she added as she put a hand to my shoulder, pulling me out of her past.

Mary said that it wasn't long ago that Jack and I were playing in her yard sunrise to sunset. Apparently I'd scream and pout because I thought the sun had fallen into the earth and was trapped. She covered her mouth briskly as she called forth the little memory, shaking her head.

The two of you would come running inside blistered with mosquito bites, your chubby faces a shade browner, she said, plunging me back into her past. When I think about you I think about Jack, she added.

I couldn't respond; there were already birds near our feet. I rotated an open palm toward the bench. Sit, I said.

When you called me, I almost didn't recognize your voice, she said, laughing. How could I—I hadn't heard from you in years, but then you sounded like your dad, when he was your age. I thought I had gone back in time! More laughter.

She agreed to speak with me out of a motherly instinct and not because of ego or anything like that, she clarified. Elders around here are asked to do cultural consultations from time to time, to impart wisdom—she figured she would help in that regard, but then it dawned on her that she had to talk about Jack, that what happened to him had to be in a book, *in mine*. The story of her life was the story of how Jack's was destroyed, she explained, her voice gently despairing. At this I winced.

I believed her. I believed that whatever Jack had endured, of which only fragments had been relayed to me, was so engrossing that it triumphed over her sense of self, that it rewired the mechanics of time such that some years, months, weeks, days, seconds became elongated, more metaphysically intrusive than others, garnering so much psychic weight that she couldn't trust chronology or linearity anymore. The days before Jack were a kind of prelude: one could skip over them and what followed would still paint a full portrait of a complicated person with dignity and stifled dreams and a cinematic breadth of emotion. Of course, love, stripped of pretense, whittled down to a matter of survivability, enticed one to abandon the autobiographical, I thought. To evoke an "I" is an elegiac act; it's to kick-start a losing game. Perhaps there's a kind of freedom in this, to be rid of the demands of personality and subjectivity and given over to a grammar of intimacy that's plural, undeniably worldly, against loneliness. Like all freedoms, however, contingency reigns. There's always the risk of disappearing into someone else, of risking one's humanity by chasing after a myth for so long you become engulfed by it, turn mythical.

Please, go on, I said, though she didn't need me to.

Mary fixed her gaze westward, perhaps on a vanishing point only she could see. It made me think of color, of the color blue; the language of her looking was deep blue. I never know where to begin, she said, worried, I wagered, not about misremembering (how could she forget?) but about how best to ratchet up sympathy, to speak in a way that didn't make use of the spoiled codes of race, codes that spelled her grandson's demise.

Maybe at the point things turned for the worse, she said, then asked, Or would that be confusing? I told her there were no rules to this, "this" being self-description, self-documentation, tasks we seldom undertake without bruising ourselves.

It was April of last year, she began. There was still snow on the ground. I remember how it melted under my slippers, how I forgot to take them off my damp feet when I went back to bed. Jack phoned me around two in the morning. No one's phone rings that late on a Saturday night unless it's bad news. By then I had already started sleeping poorly, moving in and out of consciousness until morning. I ran up the stairs as soon as I heard the ringing; it was like my body had reverted to a more agile state. *I'm driving home, Kokum*, he told me, in a hushed tone, before I could say hello. *I think a cop is following me. I've had a bit to drink, but I'm not drunk or anything. I promise. I'm on the dirt road, just before the rez.* Jack, I said, listen to me, Jack. I said his name about a dozen times during that conversation. It was all I could manage—*Jack*, she said, once more, letting it embalm us like a secret. It was an unanswered beckoning, the opposite of an incantation, a warning, something like, *Run!*

Jack swore abruptly, which always made Mary flinch, then

he put the phone away. He would leave it on speaker so that she could hear everything, but she had to keep quiet. Straightaway she discerned what she initially thought were muffled radio sounds but what was actually the deep voice of a male officer. Just then Jack turned the ignition off and suddenly there was an oppressive kind of quiet, one so simultaneously thick and porous they shared it, as if there were suddenly no distinction between where she was and where he was, as if their combined terror violated scientific law. Then, she went on, the officer opened the door and, like thunder, he started shouting again; despite being filtered through a phone, his booming speech made her jump.

Put your hands behind your head! Get down! To the ground! the officer yelled with a gravity that struck Mary again, physically, kilometers away.

Mary ran outside, unthinking, hoping Jack was closer to the house than he'd said he was, that she'd be able to see him, that the officer would know he was loved. Of course, there was nothing and no one out there. She stood in the pitch-black, her feet swallowed by snow, gripping the landline, praying Jack would be arrested peacefully. She was that hopeless—it wasn't a matter of what was horrible and what wasn't anymore. There were degrees of horror, and she learned to cope with and to live inside some of them.

A grandmother, the night droning on and on around her, awaiting what would break her heart—how else to set the scene of rural Alberta?

My whole body tensed up, she continued.

It was as if she were expecting to be shot. Or, as if Jack

being shot meant she would be too. She always worried that if Jack were to die before she did, it would be in a catastrophic fashion, from an officer's bullet, for example.

No one wants to outlive a child, no one, she said. It was a cliché that suddenly seemed new, shocking, piercing.

All Mary could do was listen, so she concentrated her sensory powers in the act of hearing. The phone was pressed so hard to her face she felt an indentation on her skin when she finally pulled it back. She heard a couple grunts, from whom she couldn't tell; for a second she didn't know if Jack was dead or alive or if his face had been shoved into the gravel or if he was kneeling there, politely, composed. They might as well have all been occurring simultaneously, she said, for she experienced a range of emotions balled up into one. Her body stopped feeling like a body. Then the connection ended. She was hung up on. She didn't budge—for how long, she didn't know. Perhaps something inside her resisted what had happened; to move would have been to surrender to reality. Had the officer used excessive force, she said, it would have been the fourth or fifth time that month that a man from the rez was unlawfully brutalized. But, of course, Jack was. He was the fourth or fifth.

I was familiar with this genre of story, in the way that all Indigenous people were familiar with it, but my body reacted as if I were hearing it for the first time. The hairs on my arms rose, as if to say, *Enough*. To whom or what does the body plead?

The image of Mary fixed like a statue in her sorrow reminded me of a line of Carl Phillips's I'd memorized: "grief, / like the dark, lifts eventually—" For her, however, the two were indistinguishable, grief and the dark. Mary, beside me, fated to account for an ongoing tragedy, the sole witness, troubled the aphorism; would the grief-dark, the dark-grief, ever dissipate? Would she ever make it to the other side of an empty night unburdened?

Jack still had his graduated driver's license, she went on, which meant he couldn't have any alcohol in his system, so he was charged with driving under the influence. His license was suspended and he was told he'd be closely monitored; any slight misdemeanor would likely result in jail time. They didn't have enough on him. They wanted there to be enough on him before they made their next move.

Mary and Jack held their breath. They were being surveilled, treated like animals. Sometimes they'd wake up and there'd be a cruiser stationed at the end of the driveway, so they'd draw the blinds, effectively forcing them to hide out all morning on their rez, in their own house.

It wasn't long ago, she reminded me, that the police outright killed Indigenous people. Across the prairies, they dumped natives in fields so that they'd freeze to death, she said with an indignation that was new to the conversation. She shivered in the late summer air as she confronted history's vastness. All they've done is try to kill us, she said.

Growing up, Mary and her siblings and cousins weren't afraid of imaginary monsters. Everywhere lurked the more realistic threat of white men whom they feared would snatch them away from their families and put them in one of the residential schools along the lake, or worse. She and my kokum were lucky, Mary explained, because they stayed home to help raise the babies. Their brothers, however, weren't. Their generation was distrustful of everyone who stared at them as if the purpose of sight were to elicit disgust. They felt as if they were being stalked and ignored at the same time. She could go on and on, she said, enumerating every injustice, every racist act that befell them, but there would be no language left inside her if she did. And what good would that do her?

It was any old weekday and we were in the middle of a genocide. No one, however, lived differently because of this, not even us, the captive and killable. Or was it that we'd never stopped running, that we couldn't distinguish between being alive and living furtively anymore? Sometimes I think there should be no art, no literature, under these conditions, that the street should be our blank page, revolution our magnum opus, love our oeuvre.

Mary thought that Jack losing his truck, his mobility, would finally force him to reckon with whatever demons he harbored. "Demons" was her word. My phrase was "the psychic life of dispossession." Mary kept feeding him the same cautionary tales, because he had no one else to be nagged by. His parents were more like acquaintances, coming in and out of his life at their leisure. They had Jack very young, at eighteen, without intention, and almost immediately broke up after he was born. There was, on the one hand, infidelity, and, on the other, an intimacy of convenience that wouldn't quite amount to love; then a baby split them apart, and they weren't able to hold up a world. Jack came under Mary's care because of this fissure, an arrangement that was supposed to be provisional. His mom and dad wanted to experiment with what was possible, as all eighteen-year-olds do, and so they fell in love with other people, built new families, fabricated new lives, and mostly, unfortunately, grew indifferent to and distant from Jack. Perhaps he was proof of a past that brought them shame in the way that only former versions of one's self can. Jack, I thought, was evidence of how permanent a wound a misplaced desire or a misfired arrow could leave behind. To be parentless—what an ordinary misfortune.

It's so easy to abandon a child, Mary said, then appeared to be momentarily bereft of words.

The blowback is asymmetrical, of course. Do the little ones ever recover from that? I thought. Would Jack? She doubted it. Sometimes she blamed herself, for not demanding more of his parents, of her own child. Sometimes she blamed the irony that those closest to you slip into blind spots inside of which they can realize an entire life.

In a similar way, Jack didn't miraculously reinvent himself after the officer's warning. No kind of intervention felt viable on Mary's part.

I don't think he's a criminal, I should clarify, she said.

At the end of the day, wasn't he just like everyone else? I thought. Wasn't he just a young man who thought he was on time's bad side, who couldn't pause to figure out what being in the world could look and feel like when separated from a sense of endangerment?

Who was she to judge anyway? Mary offered. All she'd done these last few years was live inside his anguish. Mary shifted her body, inched closer to me as she spoke. I pictured it—her body—contorted so as to be jammed inside Jack's torment, then stopped myself. What good would that image do?

She loved him as if that were all one needed to make a good life. No one can deny that, she said. Still, he drank, did drugs, disappeared for days at a time, had a new girlfriend every other week—this was his routine, his way of life. The nights he didn't come home, she would lie in his bed, bury her face into his pillow, then fall asleep out of exhaustion, hoping that when she woke up he'd be beside her or in her bed or on the couch. One night, she woke up after midnight to use the bathroom, and just as she was turning the knob, out came Jack, his pupils so enlarged and blackened she was momentarily frightened; she hadn't heard him come home. He stood up straighter, seemed taller, and his gait was something akin to floating or hovering. He didn't acknowledge her, neither with words nor a glance. It was something like a haunting, as if past, present, and future suddenly merged inside a long minute, as if he walked straight out of a nightmare of hers. Before she could say anything, he was already outside, in his truck. When she returned to bed, she envisioned kicking him out, relinquishing herself of his vices and, in this, her dread. Her sense of who she was had become so tangled in the person she perceived Jack to be that however strong the compulsion to sever ties with him was, it was always superseded by a drive to fight for him, to sacrifice her life for his. If she couldn't save him, at least she would be an audience to his struggle for glory, however loosely he defined it. When he would open up to her, which was a rare occurrence, he'd fixate on wanting to be remembered, she explained, making air quotes with two fingers when she said "remembered," but he'd never elaborate. He wanted to leave a legacy; he wanted to be someone whom people revered, either out of fear or respect, I couldn't say. *There's a difference between infamy and reverence*, I wanted to say to Mary, but I figured she already knew, instinctively, that only the living sweat over semantics.

A few days after that late-night encounter, Jack was arrested. Possession of drugs for the purpose of trafficking.

I had always suspected him of dealing, Mary said, but it was one of those things I couldn't stop him from doing. How was he supposed to get to a job thirty minutes away without a license? she asked.

As a retired community librarian, Mary subsisted mostly on a pension, so she couldn't toss money at him. Plus, employers in nearby towns like this one didn't take a chance on him; he was nothing but an untrustworthy rez kid in their eyes. He had no choice. Mary understood that. When she would chastise him, it would sometimes be without conviction, because questions of ethics are complicated here. It's not like in the city, where you are, she said. Amid this conundrum she stopped trying to will him to turn his life around. Toward what would he have aimed himself anyway? There was only him and Mary's longing, which was about him, and his rage, which was about the past. It seemed that whatever Jack did to try to be less encumbered by the world, the world would retaliate, lashing out with equal or greater force.

People like us are born with an existential debt, one we remain unfree to, I wanted to say, but the truth threatened to demolish us both with its brutal simplicity.

Clarity wounds. Clarity intrudes.

Some boys are as fleeting as the memory of rainwater during a wet spring. Many of us are relics of an impossible future, too drenched in the past to gesture to anything but loss. We are questions first and foremost, then children. Which means we are half-truths; we are where the boundary of the real intersects with that of the unreal. Children of an invisible war are essentially ghosts. Would hearing this line of thinking comfort Mary? I decided against it and for a politics of the unsaid.

That we could gallop right off the edge of the world—which is every rez in this province, in this country—and no one would notice is a blessing and a curse. Jack and I were Canadian only on paper, and otherworldly and mythic and heavy with history in every other regard. What were two brown boys dancing in the forests of northern Alberta but glistening accidents, lowercase letters scribbled down for no one to see, that somehow, against all odds, came to life? What was I if not a disobedient blur?

I wanted to ask Mary what it was like to raise a symbol that could speak and cry and snore, but I didn't wish to disrupt her narrative rhythm, I knew it was almost time for her to go. I kept my symbolic mouth shut, continued to listen with my symbolic ears.

I was tending to my lawn—it was late May—when three officers appeared with a search warrant and the chief's approval to enforce it, she said.

They found drug paraphernalia, one thousand dollars, and cocaine in Jack's truck, enough to have him arrested on the spot. Jack complied. It was a moment they had both antic- ipated with such apprehension that when it finally arrived they had exhausted their feeling power. Jack and Mary stared blankly at each other as he was shoved into the back of the cruiser, handcuffed, she explained.

I thought about something Ocean Vuong has articulated, which is that the hunted convert violence into a mundanity, into background noise. It becomes, against our will, but as a matter of survival, something as evident but suppressible as the presence of light.

They knew the police had more than enough to put him away for at least a handful of months.

He'd been at the Remand Centre in Edmonton ever since, awaiting trial.

Sometimes I still stay up late, waiting from him to come home. Then I remember he can't, she said. He can't come home.

Just as Mary was punctuating her sentence by clearing her throat, her ride approached, this time on the opposite side of the street.

I visit him at least once a month, she said as she rose, pat- ting down her jacket and pants. Saturday afternoons. You should stop in, say hi, perhaps he can help with your book. I'm sure he'd be happy to see a familiar face. I'll phone and have your name put on the list. Stop in, she said again, pleadingly.

As she walked cautiously to the curb, it occurred to me that I'd just been appointed the elegist of the family; it would be my job to lament, to infuse past lives with beauty and meaning, before a congregation of mourners who looked like me. Suddenly I became the family's writer and, in this, its historian, its coroner.

The van carrying Mary had already sped off before I realized I'd been looking the other way.

A MEMORY

When Jack was sixteen, his girlfriend at the time became pregnant. I happened to be on the rez when he got the news. From a cousin's front yard, I watched him walk out of the girl's house toward his truck, a recent gift from Mary. He pressed his head against the passenger-side window and began to sob. I looked on uneasily, because he hadn't seen me; I had turned his grief and anger public and it isn't always easy to forgive someone for doing so. I intervened, however, when he began to hit his head against the window, at first softly but then with enough force to injure himself. I ran toward him, yelling at him to stop. In my peripheral vision, I saw neighbors watching from their homes. I grabbed Jack's shoulder and said his name as gently and firmly as I could. We'd already drifted apart, were no longer childhood coconspirators, so I had no idea how he'd respond to the gesture, whether it would be too strange to allow. He did allow it, though: he fell onto my chest, and it was so unexpected I almost stepped backward. Barely perceptibly, he said, I can't be a dad, I can't be a fucking dad. I wasn't aware of the context, but I had enough of a hunch. All I could say was, I know, Jack, I know.

In the end, the child wasn't his, she'd been cheating on him. When this all came to light, I didn't ask Jack whether he felt relief. That was the wrong question. He had to do alone one of the unavoidable demands our humanness makes of us: submit to the indeterminacy of our feelings, allow them to govern us, however terrifying it is to do so.

4

PEOPLE WERE CRYING

The next morning, I walked the short distance from the hotel to the second interviewee's apartment. During my adolescence, the apartment complex had a reputation of housing those who were transitory, those who intended to leave the area after a year or two—teachers, doctors, laborers. It was located across from a church and behind it was a neighborhood full of cul-de-sacs and stretches of town homes occupied by nuclear families. Like the complex, its occupants, often single and from elsewhere, stood out in the otherwise starkly domestic environment.

It was humid out, as it often was during a prairie summer, so I was sweating considerably. I debated veering off course and finding a public washroom to wash my face in, but decided against it. There wasn't enough time. I would have to concede to my sweaty body.

After my conversation with Mary, I had returned to the hotel and slept deeply for many hours. The journey had taken a harder toll than I expected. I was at once physically depleted and intellectually invigorated. I felt obligated not to the recent past, the one I had just abandoned, but instead to a fantasy from another life. The fantasy that this novel or whatever it turned out to be would make me into a different person. Somewhere in the future I would think back on this muggy walk in the town I grew up in and avoided as much as possible since then, and I would feel gratitude. Already I felt myself resisting the possibility of any other outcome.

Noise from the neighboring units jutted through the walls of Michael's apartment. I was seated on a chair in an otherwise bare corner, facing Michael. His apartment was sparsely furnished, consisting mostly of a couch, a computer desk, and a small table positioned awkwardly beside the stove in his kitchen. Light pooled between us like a stain on the carpet.

I wanted to begin with an explanation, as if the body before Michael, in the shape of a bent exclamation point, were a kind of riddle. I told him I would be conducting interviews with a handful of folks from the area for a novel I intended to write—relatives, acquaintances, people of interest like him—and I hoped it would amount to an autobiography of a town, of rural Alberta.

At this, Michael recoiled, then squinted.

How do you intend to write both an autobiography and a novel? he asked.

I was interested in how a singular voice, when heard from a sociological distance, implicated a larger population, in how the autobiographical was rarely an individualistic mode; all of its wonder and devastation was social. I knew I couldn't articulate that interest in those terms. It would sound like nonsense to Michael, as so much of my academic writing and thinking would. I often questioned what use that language was when it alienated so many. But just as we don't get to choose who we love, as the saying goes, I don't think we get to choose which kinds of language envelop us like another layer of skin.

I believe every person is a repository of a community's memories, I said. A town speaks when its people do. I want to capture that voice. But I should clarify, I continued, I don't intend to record this interview, nor will I describe any of your biographical details. Through people like you, I want to summon an honest emotional voice.

My theoretical framework was that place governs the practice of self-fabrication. Even when we aren't alert to the force of history bearing down upon us, it's there all the same. Everyone from northern Alberta was a historian of it. What would people say if they were empowered to theorize about their happiness and misery? I wondered. If the sociological imagination was available to all of us, what kinds of truth would surface? With a novel, I wanted to architect a space where that could happen.

Inside a moment of suspense, I analyzed Michael's lips, which looked like a red smudge in the middle of his dark gray beard. It was as if someone had rubbed a wet thumb under his nose in one swift motion, as if his mouth were the work of a careless artist. All faces are still-drying paintings, I thought, when glimpsed from both ends of a long decade. I tried to picture Michael thirty, forty years ago. I wanted him to be beautiful, which meant I was okay making the present into something of a tragedy.

Michael had heard a portion of the project's premise before, when I rang him up last week at the newspaper he published, so I was puzzled by his expression of unease. I noticed then that the sleeves of his shirt were rolled up asymmetrically, one to his elbow, the other just above his wrist. I scanned the rest of him; his hair, slicked back with water, extended from his head unevenly. His clothes hung loosely from his thin frame, as if they'd just come out of the washing machine. The total effect of his appearance was that he seemed struck by a gust of wind, like someone had plucked him from the air, midfall, and sat him down in front of me.

Michael said there wasn't much he could tell me that wasn't already in print in the archives back at the office. This town isn't a literary spectacle, he explained, though I hadn't believed otherwise. Michael had reported on what mattered to the region for most of his adult life, and what mattered often had to do with mundanities and clichés. The stories he ran repeated every year. He suspected it was buried scandals and gossip I was after, he admitted, and that if this was the case the meeting should end sooner rather than later. He said this less accusingly than decisively, crossing one leg over the other. I was, however, of the opinion that a cliché could be an anchor, that it could bind us to the world, to one another.

A group of clichés is a reason to live, I said to Michael with an enthusiasm I hoped wouldn't embarrass him. Michael stared at me searchingly, perhaps turning over the sentiment in his head, investigating it for its plausibility. Was it intellectual non-sense masquerading as sympathy? Was there something more sinister beneath my performance of eagerness? Or was it something that could connect us? As if deciding against the latter, Michael said that if I wanted him to rehash the last half century of store openings and closings, of council elections and athletic achievements, of industrial developments and petty crime, he could have sent a digital file of his archive and saved me the drive up from the city.

Caught off guard by the absence of generosity in his voice, I resorted to a different register, one more exacting and emo-tional. I told him that I was the interviewer, which made him the interviewee, a position I knew he was unfamiliar with. I didn't see him as the place where local history was stored and nothing else. I wasn't driven to distinguish the sayable from the unsayable so as to be controversial. I wanted to illuminate how deeply entangled the two can become. I reminded him I too called the town home, that it followed me like a shadow, despite my having left a number of years ago. I could feel my language flickering, aching. I left when I had the chance because I wanted to save myself, I told him. I felt that to talk to those from our hometown might allow me to save myself again. My voice shook as the words leapt from my mouth. I imagined I'd have to sweep them up later. If this were the case, I continued to imagine, what if anything would a twenty-something find important enough to say to warrant making a mess?

I left so I could be as brief as any town, I added. I left so I could be as interminable too.

Silence befell us, but it was interrupted, or rather, intensified, by the faint sound of a pop song from a car stopped at a nearby intersection.

I watched Michael watch me. It was as if I had suddenly become un-blurry to him, as if the weather between us had taken a turn. Almost imperceptibly, he nodded with unblinking, serious eyes, which I took as a sign of fellow feeling or empathy or simply permission to proceed, however much ambiguity had filled up the room.

I want to talk to you about regret, I said.

I admitted to Michael that as a teenager the sight of him had felt like a second chance. Nothing about him was conventionally gay, but he pivoted away from the codes of normative masculinity in quiet ways I embellished in my mind to represent a grace I might inherit. Where most men were a kind of noise pollution, something akin to TV static, Michael was reserved, thoughtful, calculated. Those around me treated joy like a vocation, a task yielding material consequences they felt they were owed; I was fascinated by how easily Michael deviated from this script. Instead, he occupied an elegiac, non-arrogant register. This was what constituted sociality for our species, I reasoned. Even his grief was a lighthouse to a boy whose future had no shape to it.

Maybe early on I determined I didn't have to live, Michael said, in a plangent tone, I just had to be alive.

It was a difference so precise I had to close my eyes to hear it.

What drives a person to make that sort of compromise? he asked. A question he must've had to hear himself pose, had to know was inside him all along.

Michael explained that for him there were days when all that mattered was that he made it from the middle of one century to the start of another. This was because sometimes it felt like yesterday was still ahead of him. It was as if someone had taken a Polaroid of him before he was an autonomous being, but it was taking years and years to develop. Not enough light had hit the surface, so he lived like negative space. By the time he caught a peek of himself, he had already faded.

What this meant was that I was a gay man listening to a gay man who hadn't been listened to.

Why have you never formally come out? I asked.

During the summer of 1980, Michael said, I fell in love with a boy, a classmate. It happened unthinkingly, against common sense.

They had put themselves in danger. Perhaps having a "we," however fragile, to endanger empowered them to rationalize the irrational in the first place, I thought. They would lie in his bed and hold hands until dawn, nothing else. Michael would squeeze his hand so hard it went numb, but he never protested. They seldom spoke in his bedroom, he clarified. It was as if the dark made certain thoughts impossible to utter. All sensory faculties fell away except touch, the language-ness of it. In the absence of speech, he told the boy everything.

I knew what he meant. What is inside a letter if not light?

Any word or sound bursts the second it hits the air and then it shatters in our faces. We're exposed. Our honesty renders us ugly and irredeemable.

They were boys who knew only how to fail at boyhood, I thought. It was like an ethnographic spectacle. They were as afraid of being found out by each other's parents as they were of the encroaching season, Michael explained. There was a summerness to their little love. The sweat of June and July and August glistened in the smalls of their backs, was what I heard Michael saying. Did he want to put his tongue to the boy? Was he afraid it was forbidden, that it was a sheet of icy metal? Did the passage of time feel like a personal affront? Did they crane their heads toward the sky so as to believe they had been transported to another world?

Without warning, Michael said, the boy disappeared. Rumor had it his parents sent him to a conversion therapy camp a few hours away. People didn't say "gay," Michael added, afraid it was contagious, that it would sit in the air. Michael waited for him. He waited as if he were put on earth to wait. When the boy finally came back, weeks later, he was no longer a person but an outline of one, no longer flush with humanity. Michael would knock at his door and no one would answer. One evening he pounded on the door until he heard sirens in the distance, until all of him turned red and blue. Days later the boy enrolled in a high school on the other end of town, so Michael moved on. It was all he knew how to do, he said. He was still someone's child, and children didn't get to plunge into their solitude. Unless they did. The boy killed himself that winter. That's what Michael heard. At the funeral he wept and wept in the church bathroom. The truth of his death was lost in a place outside admission. He wept until he was no longer human. Like an animal, he wanted his mourning to be an enormous display. People were crying, and he was simply one of them. No one knew there was a specificity to his anguish.

Michael began to cry in the present—to mention a history of tears often had the effect of bringing someone to tears. I held his gaze. The thesis behind my project was that people turned into musical instruments when encouraged to testify about the conditions of their lives. My success hinged on my ability to endure whatever song was sung, so I listened with both eyes, with my hands clasped tightly in front of me.

People didn't kill themselves, not around here, Michael continued. No one forgot.

They remembered and remembered. It triggered something powerful in Michael, a survival instinct. Back then, he wanted to live. He wanted to live because it was the only thing expected of him.

My god, I didn't want to die, Michael said with a grimace, as if the thought were a new one, as if its newness disturbed him, challenged the bedrock of his worldview. Perhaps he

wasn't ready to live differently in the wake of that sort of rev-
elation, to ask more of himself. You know, he went on, that
dead boy is more proof of my continued existence than anything else.

Do we make ourselves into tragedians trying to accrue
proof of our aliveness in retrospect? I thought. Somewhere between love and loss we pitch a tent from which we
only look backward.

Was it then that you decided you wouldn't come out? I asked.

Yes and no, Michael answered.

It was a slow buildup of small decisions made in haste.

I didn't shun the gay parts of myself for good, if that's
even possible, he said.

He always deferred the day he would get the fuck out.
With age, immobility turned out to be something he didn't
have to resist anymore; it gave him context, which he thought
he had irreversibly forfeited. The future stopped feeling like
something solid thrashing against him.

The generations that preceded his were socialized to
believe homosexuality was a crime. It was only removed from
Albertan criminal law two years after he was born, in fact.
The sentiment didn't magically vanquish when reform happened. Heterosexuality was where identity began and ended.
So much so that when the AIDS epidemic ravaged gay communities all over the world, the town caught only bits and
pieces of the circumstances. What made its way out here,
north of the last major city, was enough to piece together an
intoxicating myth of gay impurity. To be gay was to be dead
or dying. Worse, to harbor the ability to kill. It became easier

for Michael to clock in and out of his body than to confront the heaviness of his desires. He was unsure what devastation they might unleash.

At some point, I thought, he convinced himself he was a stray bullet that silence had clenched between its teeth. Perhaps he was thankful for his captor.

Michael's story reminded me of Judith Butler's observation that we sometimes choose to stay attached to what injures us rather than gamble with what it might feel like to be in the world without the attachment. The psychological investment is so large it seems counterintuitive to relinquish it, regardless of its consequences. We don't want to lose too much, to be left with so little.

I was also reminded then of the story of Yellowknife's arsenic. There are currently 237,000 metric tons of arsenic in the mines near Yellowknife. For decades, men hunted gold and, by extension, happiness, another world. Left unchecked, the arsenic levels skyrocketed and seeped into the snow, into the surrounding environment, so it had to be locked away. If chemicals escaped the chambers in which they have been frozen, all biological life would cease to exist. Don't we all tell ourselves that what's inside us, our wanting, is annihilative to this degree? Don't we all suspect our most volatile yearnings, when freed from the pits of our stomachs, could upend a world? What if desire were one of the few forces that troubles the idea of continuums, meaning we're either entirely absorbed or wrecked by it? We all have it in us to destroy ourselves.

Michael produced his own analogy. He mentioned the

method of disembodied writing, where the writer is made invisible. It's an approach he trusts, because it doesn't paint a target on himself or his staff. It occurred to him the other day that we sometimes practice a kind of disembodied living.

Like a ghost trying to accentuate its ghostliness, he said, chuckling. It appears I have mastered the art!

To remain, I thought, to settle down, to stay put, meant that the act of being inhibited, of being forestalled, became the larger ebb and flow of life. Isn't geographical fate, then, nothing but an obstacle one has to surpass? If a home were a monument to what you lost or were losing out on, wouldn't you run away?

I felt compelled to reel Michael back into the room. To keep us both from wandering too long in the abstract. Did you ever fall in love again? I asked. At the abruptness of the question Michael turned his head away from me and toward a wall empty but for a degree from an online institution. I reminded him he could pass on any question that discomfited. He smiled.

Not exactly, no, he said.

Throughout the nineties he had the habit of driving down to Edmonton on weekends to try to breach the prison of indecision and regret he made of himself. He would linger at a gay bar until one or two in the morning, terrified of running into someone he knew—which never happened, he clarified. All he wanted was to be seen in a place where exposure was a kind of currency rather than a death wish. Men made advances, most of which he rebuffed. He accepted a blow job here and there in bathroom stalls but no one had names, including him.

He thought about staying in Edmonton, but, in the end, he'd lost the power to be anything but complacent, self-sacrificial. Most importantly, though, even in his thirties and forties, he felt haunted by his first and only love. The thing about memory is you can't extinguish it. It's as automatic as the spinning earth. He decided it would be wrong not to be as close to that history as possible, as if it were a dying language only he could speak. His love for the boy was so contested and fraught and tragic he was still awash in it. The emotional intensity was enough to last a lifetime.

Is that bizarre? Michael asked. That such a brief experience of love was too much?

For a second I thought Michael expected an answer from me. His eyes were pleading, but whose wouldn't be? Who wouldn't burn themselves in the drama of self-documentation? How could anyone hold such a jagged memory up to the light and not wince?

I decided against letting the interview naturally dissipate and asked Michael if he'd ever felt empty, like something vital was missing, to which he said emptiness wasn't something to run from. We all begin with emptiness, he argued: an empty name, an empty house, an empty life.

Mine is a life of beginnings, he said. Every morning I start over.

He said he doesn't ruminate on what his life could have been. It's his small act of refusal, his silent rebellion. Maybe when he looked in the mirror, he saw who he was, which was someone who was running out of time. All those years of evading death were preparatory. Without knowing it, he was practicing death, a ritual unto itself. Just then he closed his eyes, not in an effort to abate tears but as if succumbing to exhaustion. So I did too. For a short while we were alone in a shared world where nothing needed to be said or seen to grasp the other's emotional possibility.

Michael walked me to the elevator and then to the front entrance. I thanked him for his time, for his candor and vulnerability, to which he said it was nice to get things off his chest, that I could follow up if need be, that I knew where to find him. At the edge of the parking lot, I turned back to get one last look at him. Because it was five o'clock and the sun gave him a new face, or because I was twenty-four and lonely in a country that made me feel like a shipwreck, I wanted to kiss him. Instead, I said goodbye for a second time.

Back in my hotel room, it was as if I could still hear desire clamoring inside Michael. It was like a bird's wings rattling against a cage—a beautiful and terrible melody I suspected he would eventually die to.

•

Suppose a body were trapped between two parentheses, I thought, made out to be an aside, a distraction, a trace of another narrative possibility. Would you set it free, set it loose on the world?

5

YEARS AND YEARS

I'd never had sex in rural Alberta. The entirety of my erotic life had played out in cities across Canada, but predominantly in Edmonton. Anonymous sex and one-night stands, which characterize the vast majority of my sexual experiences, rid the lust-object of biographical depth, so I also couldn't confidently say I'd been with someone who had similarly been a self-loathing homo in a small town, though perhaps that was more likely than not, Edmonton being something of a gay refuge in the prairies. Like others, when I moved to the city I needed the dirt shoveled out of me with human hands. I had to learn, however, that a man at work could be mistaken for so much when in actuality he meant very little. It meant he was counting down the hours and minutes and seconds until he was unobligated. A bed wasn't always an extension of the future. Two nameless men rattling around in the dark sometimes just made each other dimmer and dimmer. I didn't question myself, didn't think twice before I knocked on a door in a part of the city I'd never been to. I was a regular accident, entranced by my capacity to be disfigured by a hope that, once fired, would produce a kickback. What I made was derivative, but it shimmered nonetheless. I faced each new man with the same unwavering belief that he would wrench me from my past and save me from a life of rotten solitude. It never occurred to me that this could take place in northern Alberta.

Was rural sex different than urban sex, if such things could be said to exist? "Maybe love really does mean the submission of power," Carl Phillips wrote in *Reconnaissance*. To what powers would I have to submit? When it was all over, would I want to burn the bed? Or would the memory be an infinite summer?

That these questions coaxed a middle-aged white man to my hotel room was damning proof of my willingness to abandon a principled ethnographic praxis. His name was Graham and he enunciated it as if it were one syllable, without vowels: Grhm. Per Grindr he was fifty-three feet away, which stirred me into an irrational alertness. I peered through the hole on the door, lifted the curtain slightly to scan the parking lot, swung the closet door open. Upon our exchanging face pictures (neither of us wanted to fully expose ourselves on the three-by-three grid) and sexual preferences (I, a bottom who pretended to be vers; he, a top who at times dabbled in butt stuff; both practitioners of safer sex, both into extended foreplay), he took the elevator two floors down. It was that transactional, economical; we were two panting commodities, out of place, in transit.

He also exhibited a general degree of civility during our short conversation that suggested he wouldn't catfish or murder or catfish-murder me. (There were clues one could look for: the angle at which one took photos of their face and the quality of said photo, for example.) Seldom did I turn a man down after agreeing to meet on the app. Engaging in countless random hookups with countless random men had the effect of drawing out the arbitrariness of sexual taste; all arousal required was thin context, an excess of which Grindr traded in. Mostly I wasn't taught to say no, mostly my body was a question for which any man could be an answer, a solution, dead air to float inside of. Something inside me dilated like a pupil at the sight of a shame-drenched man. Unlike a sentence, my body didn't end; I was an elastic form inside which men actualized their inner consciousnesses. When you think of me, picture a glistening wreck, something of a piece with the subliminal. The thing about the sublime is that at some point you have to look away.

•

Graham was sizing me up as I undressed.
I had awkwardly placed my right hand on the computer desk
to balance,
a clumsy maneuver he interpreted as a plea,
so he squatted to pull my tight pant legs off one after the other,
a moment of spontaneous and outsized tenderness
that both of us could only recognize with a laugh.
He, already naked, presented me with his non-digital body,
which was measured only against my idiosyncratic catalog of
previous lovers,
information that was unavailable to him in the same way his
was to me;
we got off on each other's unavailabilities,
more aroused by what we didn't know
than by the bits of data fed to us on the app as unerotic statistics.
For all he knew, I was a small town he could get lost inside of;
for all I knew, he was a cliff I could hurl myself from.
We stepped rhythmically toward each other,
as if about to begin a choreographed dance;
seen from the point of view of the door,
one might mistake our embrace for a sadder sight,
that of Graham teetering by himself to the sound of nothing.
What we were: two bodies pulsating inside a co-constituted
indeterminacy.
What we weren't: real, realized, finished.
What he said: here are some words, swallow them.

No, he didn't say that, but his dick did swell against mine;
he grabbed both with his hand and stroked them as if
masturbating.
Here's a myth:
two men, joined at the crotch, moaning
in a town neither called home.
I dragged my cheek down his hairy chest,
which was wet like a layer of condensation on a window;
as if he were a window, I pressed my face into him and
opened my eyes;
I took him inside my mouth and he held his palm at the back
of my head;
he pushed me forward, as if to throw me against himself.
Calmly, he lay down on the bed;
I crawled over him, upside down,
such that our mouths were at opposite ends of each other,
an image that always made me think
of a tree gnarled around another simply because it is there,
proximal.
We were there, proximal.
Once upon a time we were trees for an entire night.
I hoisted myself up, rotating one hundred and eighty degrees
in order to kiss him,
which was a way of tasting myself.
My arms gave out and I crashed down onto him.
Kaboom, I said.
He winced melodramatically, contorting his face
as if he had just been unexpectedly blinded;
interpreting this as a cue, he reached over to the bedside table

to grab the condom I had waiting there.

I squirted lube onto my palm;

he rolled the condom on.

I hovered over his groin, reaching behind myself for his dick,

then I pushed downward softly, grimacing at the added

pressure.

Once we made a rhythm we settled into, I couldn't help

but hum;

either Graham didn't notice or didn't care, because it went

unremarked-upon,

but I wanted his memories of me to be sonic as much as they

would be fleshy;

it was how I said: *I'm a person, I have agency.*

I'm close, I'm close, he warned;

I dismounted and lay beside him, pointing to my torso.

He tore off the condom and took aim with concentration,

emptying onto me

with a forcefulness that to some might look like a sob,

then, as if to bow, he lowered his head to my waist,

slowly, methodically, he licked the semen from my stomach,

which was a way of tasting the world.

·

I resisted the urge to run my hand through Graham's hair,
for it was thin and had receded at his temples; his aging was
imprinted on his skull, which made me think of the rings
inside a tree's trunk. It seemed counterintuitive to pour him
back into his ordinary body, which would rupture the post-

sex tranquility that had blanketed us, the effect of which was to make one feel bodiless. Instead, I laid my head on his chest again, as if to listen for his heartbeat. With an index finger I traced a second little heart over his right pectoral muscle.

Now you have two, I said.

Why do I need two hearts? he shot back, craning his neck downward to rummage for my gaze.

Most wouldn't question it, most would be grateful, I answered.

You said you're here for work—what do you do? I asked. A question most askable during a Grindr encounter after ejaculation. The minutiae of our daily lives are so unsexy.

I'm an engineer, for an electrical company. First time out here. The guy who usually does this is on vacation, so I had to fill in. Nothing strenuous, though, mostly just sitting at a computer, going over numbers. I don't want to bore you, he said, interrupting himself, then he kissed my forehead softly.

He told me there was something magical or enigmatic about me in a tone I assumed was meant to indicate a kind of shrewdness.

Tell me about *you*, he said.

It was past midnight.

I rubbed my neck with my hand, inadvertently brushing against his armpit and causing my nose to take in its scent, which I'd somehow remained ignorant of or had simply suppressed, integrated into the olfactory world of the hotel room. Now it coursed through my body, down toward my feet, as if pulled by gravity. I was taxidermied by it.

Graham hugged me, interlacing his hands over my rib

cage. His grip was tight but unmenacing, which is to say it was questionless. For a second I thought: Is it possible to be caressed to death? For another: If I could repeat each day in this configuration, a novel would be of no use to me. From the corner of my eye, however, I spotted the hidden truth of the gesture. Without knowing it, he was tugging at the third finger on his left hand.

I'm a novelist—wish I could say it was a temporary gig, that I'd resume a normal, uncomplicated life after a few days away, I joked. But, alas, I'm cursed with the conviction that I have it in me to unearth something interesting about the human condition, I continued. I said "human condition" as if it were the title of an Oscar-winning film or a terminal illness that hadn't befallen anyone I knew. It wasn't, however, incorrect to say that I suffered from the Human Condition, that I would die without having written down everything I could about being alive.

Graham widened his eyes. You're not going to write about me, are you? he said, without nervousness, maybe acting out the norm that one should object to being written about, a norm about which he was indifferent. Just change my name and identifying features, if you do, he added, then kissed me again, this time on the lips. The kiss was nondescript, neither emptied of nor vibrating with intimacy. It was akin to a handshake, as if he were introducing himself to me for the first time, perhaps a consequence of having now embedded himself in a narrative over which he knew he held little dominion. Perhaps he felt it more important to be misrepresented than not represented at all.

You don't need to worry about that, I reassured him. The book already has a shape; everything would be put into disarray to insert you into it.

Everything? he asked, visibly amused.

Everything, I said, invisibly amused.

This roused Graham's competitive spirit. I'm not offended, he said, but it sounds like you don't believe I have anything compelling to add, no insight to impart?

That's not what I meant! Okay, okay, I said.

I let the silence build up between us, mulling over what to say next. I dug my face into his neck, so that my voice would be muffled, less interrogative than impish.

Tell me about the invisible wedding ring you keep fiddling with, I said.

Graham shot up, causing my face to plummet into the damp spot where his back had been strewn. Before he could let the terror of speculation wash over him, I continued, still muffled: It's an assumption; I saw a few minutes ago, your hands, that is.

If he left right now, I'd be a monument to humiliation, a private landmark that would exist solely in our shared geographies of the past.

Graham placed his hands over my ears, as if to block out a harsh noise, then tilted my head upward. His facial expression morphed from incredulity into curiosity.

Clever boy, he said at last.

In most of my sexual forays with men over thirty, I was cast as "boy," which brought into focus an ethical ambiguity I seldom wanted to wade into. I fled from that spoiled subjectivity, defenseless. Behind him, the headboard shook, highly susceptible to his language, a condition I shared with it.

My eye line was flush with his flaccid dick. Our asymmetry was a gesture toward beauty.

My wife's name was Sara, he said at last, not solemnly as one might expect, but with an air of indifference, proof that "Sara" had already been routed away from his circuits of identification. I could have correlated the flat tone with his character, but it seemed more probable that it had to do with one of the conditions of the one-night stand: he could give everything to me, years and years of everything, because he would never thereafter have to face down the debris in my cupped hands.

She moved to the town in which Graham grew up outside Grande Prairie, one not much larger than this, the summer before they started high school, he said.

They dated straightaway, as they were two middle-class white kids for whom dating was what granted them access to a semi-stable identity and, with it, social legibility. They didn't know how to be individuals yet; to be in a relationship was second nature. They knew themselves by way of what others desired about them.

Anonymous sex was tantalizing partly insofar as it allowed for a suspension of individuality that made it possible to be a non-person given over to an animalistic urge. Perhaps this sort of metaphysical ambivalence was always the precondition for Graham's sense of self.

He explained that one foot was in the realm of self-making and the other was tied to Sara, so much so that their footsteps seemed to be synchronized, that one couldn't make do without the other. They got stuck in that state of suspension, of half-knowing and blind ignorance. It was like daydreaming continuously, which, to my mind, was the easiest way for teenagers to inhabit the world, deliriously. Everyone accommodated their simple joy, its indistinct racket, he said. They continued to step in rhythm; there were no missteps, no bumps. When they both enrolled at the University of Alberta, they moved into a one-bedroom apartment on the edge of campus, and their families blended without much effort, as did their aspirations and losses and worldviews. For a long time, it seemed preordained; they were proof that fate didn't always leave people stranded. They married the autumn after convocation, Graham went on. To surprise her, he wrote his own vows.

Graham stared at the window even though the curtains blocked out the night sky. He couldn't, I presumed, bear to look at anyone, at any living thing.

I can't remember what I said word-for-word, he said finally, straightening his back, but what I can recall is that I said we'd inhaled each other's breath for five years, that it was a thrill I didn't want to ever get used to.

The world was easier to say yes to, he went on. Every morning he woke up next to her was a resounding yes. Every kiss, every inside joke, every stolen glance, was a yes that roared from him. Graham said he'd only known how to be in a body, how to move and think, as an extension of Sara. He was hers at an existential and cellular level.

I was stunned. Graham evidenced a poetic instinct I hadn't expected he was capable of.

I remember looking over at my dad and he was crying, he continued, which was strange to me, not just because I had never seen him cry before, but also because Sara wasn't. I didn't think much of it, because who hunts for clues of a doomed marriage at the altar?

Graham said it was like the wedding unearthed an unfixable misalignment; their "I dos" came from different places. Hers was something of a relinquishment of possibility, which he never could have guessed at. Love, he realized, can be oppressive simply because it illuminates everything one has turned their back on.

A romance of the negative, I hadn't said.

For months he watched Sara recoil from his touch. It was as if in response to his description of love as a kind of exchange of breath, she held hers in, kept it from him. In the end all he could do to keep them both from going mad was break things off. He was sure she would plunge into her sadness and solitude and build the most pathetic life at their depths before she'd divorce him, before she'd betray everything the social contract of marriage stands for. As they were finalizing the divorce, she finally admitted she realized he wasn't strictly heterosexual and, because of this, worried she would never last as the primary recipient of his sexual attention. She caught his eyes darting at men, which was automatic by then, a habit. It fucked her up. Burrowing into him on the couch, something they'd done innumerable times, became unbearable, Sara confessed to him. Something that hadn't happened, something that existed solely as potential, this was what ended their short marriage. Everything they had done, their once-effortless "us," none of that could square up against the enemy that is the future. She thought what I had done to her was an act of cruelty, he said. But, really, I would've stayed with her for the rest of my life. There was a lot I didn't know, but I knew that with total certainty.

Graham put his hand into mine, then said he couldn't deny how fun it had been to experiment sexually, that he was fortunate to have found the beds of men like me. I wanted this to be less damning than it was. I felt indicted by it, squished. This is how it always happens, he continued. In a hotel room, with complete strangers. I live in the house Sara and I purchased together. Our wedding photos still hang on the walls. I guess something inside me still resists rupturing that old life, even if it's just an illusion these days.

How long would Graham live with that degree of distance from his true desires? I wondered. Repression comes as naturally to some as breathing, I reminded myself. Indeed, much of my adolescence was spent estimating how much or little of myself I would have to render invisible in order not to gravely expose my otherness. Graham could settle into the rhythm that had already begun to form and never see the ways it was deleterious. To him, that would be what constituted a sexual and romantic life. He might never think to question it.

As for me, at twenty-four I wasn't any more emotionally enriched than he was. To end up in love and safe and in a happy marriage—I would have to get to the other side of a great deal of suffering first. That felt as inevitable to me as literature.

He could say more, I assumed, but I didn't want him to. I

didn't know what to say either, so I rolled my speechless body onto his. We fucked again and then another time, both agreeing to make with our bodies a cathedral of distraction. What this meant was that I was fated to want again and again to undertake the work of finding in a man a beautiful landscape for which there was no evidence of its existence.

INTERLUDE

ART

I'd been in the bathtub for almost an hour, but the smell of sex and displaced yearning still hung in the air. Flowing through me were the shock waves of intercourse: the euphoria of surrender, the catatonia of regret. An incitement to abstract thought as powerful as any.

I was reading *Água Viva*, and in it Clarice Lispector wrote: "Writing is the method of using the word as bait." If nothing else, I thought, art could usher in a brief trace of another kind of embodiment, another experience of having a body that wasn't already absorbed into the misery machine called *life under white supremacist capitalist heteropatriarchy*. At the very least, it could do what sex did for me, give access to what Lispector called "whatever is not word," what I believed to be another way of saying "the opposite of the present."

●

I felt an urge to text River. I reached for my phone perched dangerously on the toilet and wrote: *Inside my body it was loud like a body, or a city street.* To which they responded: *O, desire!*

●

So what if the present was an empty bathroom inside which I shivered, at least I had something to write about.

●

I was thinking about something an ex-boyfriend told me about clouds: how on overcast days, towns and cities heat up, if only slightly, because the warm air becomes trapped. It made me reconceptualize all the sadness in my body, made me wonder if it, like heat, floated up from my stomach and chest and pressed against the roof of my skull. Late one night, in bed, I asked that ex to press his hand to my head:

Feel anything? I asked.

No, he said.

It's all gone to my head, I said.

What has? he asked.

I spoke with such conviction and self-awareness I wasn't compelled to clarify.

•

Let's say art turns us all into fatigued metaphysicians.

Let's say the novel makes only one provocation it can't actualize: Prove to me with certainty the present is all there is.

Let's say I'm fictitious in the way reality is fictitious.

Let's say I have to be unendingly invented and reinvented.

Let's say I believe in myself the way a good citizen believes in the goodness of his country.

Let's say that's a lie.

Let's say I can't be a beautiful sentence unto myself.

Let's say I hate this about myself.

Let's say I'm drowning and I'm in a hotel room.

Let's say this is a simple story with a beginning and an end.

Let's say I'm part of a breathtaking view.

Let's say I made love and art as if I hadn't already lost the war.

•

A couple years ago, I'd fallen in love with a man on a short-term visa in Canada. This was in my early days of queer dating when any man could become synonymous with the future. I adored him with a desperation that has become not just foreign to me but dangerous. I was simply someone with whom he could pass the time. He left unspoken the problem of temporality, which was a mathematical one, meaning we didn't add up to something long-lasting. Nonetheless, or perhaps driven to disprove what he experienced as a statistical truth, I went on for months in a fiction of stability I couldn't figure out how to make real. I told myself I'd move to his home country, would leave everything I ever knew behind. We were, in the end, just two people made up of two other people. Nothing more. When he left, I stopped writing, stopped caring about art. Months later I expected all my relationships to end in devastation, an old character flaw the thought of which devastates me still. I needed to learn how to live and love without placing an embargo on creativity.

•

Slowly, the water disappeared into the overflow drain. I pulled the plug in order to let the rest go (to where, I wasn't sure). With melodrama, I stood up, tilted my head, hammered it into the air, said, *Here, take this too!*

A MEMORY

During the second year of my first degree, I rented a two-bedroom apartment in downtown Edmonton that I could barely afford with the monthly allowance sent by my reserve, because to be downtown was to be in the center of something solid and engrossing. In those initial years, I'd felt disoriented and listless. I was struggling to unlearn the habits of my rural upbringing: to be at peace with not knowing what was where, with only talking to a few people any given week. My view of the city was still that of a visitor's, of someone who'd soon leave. I'd intended to seek out a roommate, but after seventeen years of cohabitation I found an almost intoxicating pleasure in living alone that I didn't want to surrender. My apartment was essentially empty, save for a couch my aunt had given me and the mattress and furnishings I hauled with me from my childhood bedroom. I had purchased a large overhead lamp from a department store and I treated it like a work of art. It was proof I could externalize some aspect of my internal world, a task I brought a deep seriousness to.

One weekend, I got a call from Jack, which was rare, in fact it hadn't happened since high school. He'd just been fired for smoking weed on the job and he'd just been broken up with for not being emotionally available. He was sick of his life, he told me. He needed a fresh start, someplace where he was more than what others assumed about him, and he knew I had space. I said yes because he was a native boy on the run from history.

Unsurprisingly, history tailgated him all the way to the city. Right away, he was hired to move stock at Walmart in a minimum wage position and I drove him there and back on the days and nights he didn't have enough gas to transport himself. After two weeks, he was overworked and depressed. I seldom saw him, other than in transit. When he was at the apartment, he slept. When he wasn't working, he was in parts of the city I never visited. He fell in with folks for whom sociality was an extension of a drunken night or the next day's hangover. Neither of us could see that he was inside his grief so intensely it colored his perception of the city. I watched at a distance, as if from a perspectival point outside the present, as I was still barely a person myself. Before the month's end, Jack had quit his job and returned to northern Alberta. He'd been texting another girl, one he'd flirted with before. He said he had to see through the possibility of being with her and that he was sorry he couldn't help me out with the rent or groceries at all. I didn't make a fuss about it, because I too desperately believed that if anything would save two Cree boys from the throes of a world that wasn't built for them it would be love and little else.

6

MOTHERHOOD

All morning I thought about Toni Morrison—an ongoing activity since her death. I had just read an article Dionne Brand wrote in memoriam, in which she said that Morrison "changed the texture of English itself." Many whom I follow on social media posted notes of grief spun in tribute to the vitalizing force that made Morrison the greatest writer of our time. Earlier in the year, I'd watched the documentary about her writing life, *The Pieces I Am*, and as I listened to the audiobook of *Sula* while driving to visit my mother, I was reminded of the poet Sonia Sanchez's deep emotivity, of how radically affected she was by Morrison's life and work. Morrison changed how we mourn too, in that "literature" and "mourning" could be of a piece with an exercise of freedom against the pervasiveness of racism. When I first caught wind of the news I cried outside in the rain. For once, I wanted to be vivid, like a metaphor, like weather.

My mother hadn't engaged with Morrison's work until that afternoon, when I read to her one of the author's oft-cited aphorisms: "We die. That may be the meaning of life. But we do language. That may be the measure of our lives." My mother repeated, "But we do language," let it permeate the campground she'd been staying at with her husband for the last week (a ritual of theirs that had to do with a performance of leisure and relaxation as middle-class ideals and therefore chores). Did my mother think of herself as someone who did language? Somehow I couldn't ask her. There were days I felt pummeled by language, when I was unable to write anything, and I assumed this was something I inherited from her.

Many of the books I'd been moved by over the last year were about motherhood. This didn't occur to me until I found myself grappling with the figure of the mother in my dissertation: "A mother is a library seconds before the tornado strikes," I wrote. Seldom have I felt like a motherly figure, so it wasn't from experience that I wrote this sentence. Maybe it had to do with a desire to stage a drama of conversation with my own mother, one that even now I wince at the prospect of, even when I've rationalized it as "research." In Roland Barthes's *Mourning Diary*, a son is unmoored from the pleasures of worldliness in the wake of his mother's death: "I limp along through my mourning," he wrote. "Since I've been taking care of her, the last six months in fact, she *was* 'everything' for me, and I've completely forgotten that I'd written. I was no longer anything but desperately hers." For me, motherhood was a forest I rarely wandered into. And when I did, I wasn't a careless tourist; I exited by nightfall. If I was ever "desperately hers," it was while inside the womb.

She told me once that when she found out she was pregnant with me she cried tears of gratitude. She'd gone through a miscarriage the year before and realized she was desperate to have a child even though she was still quite young. For months, she didn't tell anyone about the pregnancy, worried that the same outcome would befall her. It was the most superstitious time of her life, she'd said. I was undeniably a part of her, as her growing stomach evidenced, but she also felt that I was barely there. It was a period marked by agony and hope, by the agony of hope. This all felt incredibly distant now, both in terms of time passed and the emotional rift that had opened between us.

My mother and aunt moved in together when my dad passed away. (I have no memory of him; I was barely two years old.) My aunt, Donna, was as much a maternal figure to me as anyone could be. Because she was younger, she was regularly home when my mother was out working or socializing.

At some point, my mother decided that the men she dated wouldn't interact with me until she met her current partner, which meant that there were chunks of my childhood in which she didn't exist.

I was an evidently gay teenager (my flamboyance was subtle, but it was flamboyance all the same), though no one had a language gentle enough to inform me I could still be happy, so my sadness was always visible. When I did finally come out, my mother didn't say anything; she disappeared for a few days. Donna was left to keep me from falling apart. We watched *Brokeback Mountain* the next day and she hugged me as I sobbed during the ending. Their tragedy felt resonant. It'd be years before I severed myself from the trope of gay catastrophe; I still found myself falling back into that way of thinking now and then.

For a long time, I couldn't wholeheartedly trust my mother. It turns out I still didn't know how to ask her how we begin to heal.

Some nights my pseudo-motherlessness seemed to me a more animal form of freedom; other nights I felt corroded by it, like a sculpture long severed from the fingers of its maker. Barthes rebelled against the possibility of becoming his "own mother." He wrote entry after entry refusing the imposition of that sort of subjectivity, denying it the status of a fatalism. This metaphysical and metaphorical state, however, was the condition of possibility for my selfhood; it was a beginning that begot other beginnings. This was the power parents held over us, that of shaping the kinds of debt we carried into our own adulthoods. That we all haul little five- and ten-pound dumbbells of the past around and say nothing of it is a kind of poetry.

What this severance from a traditional notion of motherhood opened up to me was a closeness with a queerer notion of motherhood. I was mothered by biological kin as well as by friends and lovers and strangers and myself. This was what I suppose the writer Maggie Nelson means by the "democratization of the maternal function," a more egalitarian distribution of the labor of caretaking, less a gendered burden and more so a collective undertaking that is reciprocal. We are both caring and cared for. Mothering is about being with others in a context in which mutual flourishing is a shared goal. The culmination of this practice was the making of a world in which no one was imprisoned in their solitude. Take my friendship with River as an example; I became the person I am in their company. Who I am is tied to who they are. In this way, we have a kind of collective self, and we tend to it as one does a garden. That, to me, is the mark of the maternal function.

Still, I loved my mother with the fortitude of a line break. She was a quaking "I" about to leap, like a doe that's suddenly no longer a symbol, into the future. I knew it wasn't my job to catch her, to be a comma or a period, only to trudge now and then toward wherever she landed so that she might say to someone: *You made it.*

She stood firmly in her small frame as she rolled out the canvas from the fifth-wheel to architect a temporary refuge from the midday sun. Her hair was characteristically volumized, shaped around her face like parentheses. I was struck, as was often the case, with the totality of her appearance, a prettiness she hadn't passed down to me. It had the effect of drawing out what was an already long-drawn-out sense of alienation. We asked very little of each other, guarded each other's peace and solitude when we did come together, which is Rilke's trusted definition of love. What my mother hadn't said made up a non-autobiography that haunted me. Haunting not in the sense of being terrorized, but a haunting that's ever-present yet opaque, a thick fog, something one can learn to grow used to. Small talk was the arena inside which we performed an allegiance to our discarded pasts and still-to-be-determined futures. I wanted to ask her everything: *Where were you? What is your definition of love? What sort of person were you in your twenties? What is there to apologize for? What do we do now?* To an extent, the novel couldn't exist without her voice, her confessions and mythologies of the self, but with each passing minute I felt with greater inevitability that our silences would protract. As she tidied, began preparations for a barbecue she was set to host that night for coworkers, I thought of Kogonada's *Columbus* and how I watched it breathlessly. I waited for there to be a volatile confrontation between the protagonists and their respective parents (either in the past or the present), parents who so empirically diminished their child's happiness in the name of their own world-engulfing desires. It didn't arrive, but an emotional relinquishment did take place, the subtext of which was that we don't have to be the bearers of a family's pessimism. Only steps away from the large body of water I regularly visited as a teen, afraid I would never be as expansive as it was, I could've broken my vow of silence, stepped out from the taillights of her indifference, and waited to quarrel in the ditch of our shared history. I was, however, already bruised; I didn't want to throb any more intensely, didn't want the past to pool at my feet more than it already had. It was the end of summer, and I was no longer a boy.

•

Rachel Cusk wrote: "That's writing for you: when you make room for passion, it doesn't turn up." What I'm saying is, that's writing for you: when you make room for your mother, she doesn't turn up. What does: a brief scene, a little pathos, the ringing earth.

An account of one's mother will always be imperfect and imprecise, so I was determined to zero in on the beautiful facets of imperfection, to make monuments of what was misarticulated, left unarticulated, sites to revisit when I worried I hadn't said or done enough to abolish any residual anger, hadn't painted a portrait of us resonant with both grace and heartbreak. Maybe one day I'll write my own mourning diary using a vocabulary of life and death I don't yet have access to. Maybe my mother will too. We will weave narratives of joy in which no one toes the edge of another's existential fault line and calls it kinship.

If there were a transcript of the entirety of my human experience to date, how much of it, I wondered, would be underlined by readers? It was possible none of it would be, a gentler outcome than the reverse. How cruel, to live a life unhinged from meaninglessness, I thought, as I watched through the windshield as my mother pressed her face into her husband's chest.

•

As I pulled out of the campground and back into adequate cell service, I decided to call Donna, the only person who could help me make sense of my inability to address my mother's past. The phone rang and rang, and as I was about to hang up her voice finally came through.

Hello, dear, she said. It's been ages since I've heard from you. You know I worry about you all the time, all alone in the city.

I'm back home, actually, I said. It was last-minute. I'm here to do research for this book I want to write.

I'm not around, she said disappointedly. The last time I saw you was your birthday. Let me take you to bingo next time I'm in the city. You're my good-luck charm, you know?

Yes, Auntie, I said. That sounds like a great idea. Where are you, by the way?

We're camping in Jasper. The kids are zip-lining with their dad as we speak. I'm much too old for that white-people nonsense. Creator didn't put me on earth to be barreling through the sky.

We laughed deeply and freely, the sort that makes the world feel at least marginally more habitable.

So, she went on, is there something bothering you? Even your laugh sounds a little unlike you.

I was just at Mom's campsite, I said. I meant to ask her a few questions, maybe about her childhood and what it was like to give birth to me and lose Dad so soon after.

Donna sighed. That's hard, she said.

Yes, I agreed. Hence why I wasn't able to breach the subject at all, I said.

Your mom's never been one to open up about her feelings, let alone about the past. I always thought that people who've come from hardship either never stop talking about what they've been through or don't talk about it at all. She really loved your dad. The sadness consumed her. I was young then, and even I could see it.

Donna's voice softened, became more solemn. Her voice set in this register always put me on the verge of tears.

I moved in with her shortly afterwards, she continued. Kokum said I had to, that I didn't have a choice in the matter. Your mom had a lot of grief to bear and so much living to do; she was only in her early twenties. She and I haven't discussed this time either, but what I believe is that she was dealing with at least two kinds of depression, postpartum and in response to the death. She didn't have the capacity to mother herself, let alone you.

Truthfully, I thought, I harbored anger about that, and I blamed her. But a few years back I had this sudden epiphany, about when I started learning more about racism in northern Alberta and colonialism more broadly, that my feeling of motherlessness had also to do with history. My mother was at the whim of forces she couldn't always see or name.

I do think she carries shame about that time, Donna

said. I took on parenting duties, which came natural to me, thankfully. I changed diapers, did laundry, made milk bottles, cooked, all before my first kiss. People thought I was your mom when I took you to the playground, though I never told your mom about that. Do you think you should tell her that you forgive her?

Honestly, I don't know. I don't want it to open up old wounds, though perhaps they've never closed. I feel like I've done enough self-care and inner work that I'm no longer burdened by what goes undisclosed. What I think I want is to see her in her totality. I want to know her side of the story without feeling personally implicated. I don't want to be too vulnerable to what she has to say.

That time will come. I'm not sure when, she said, but you might have to let her decide.

I would've asked her the wrong questions today, anyway, I think. On that note, can I ask you something?

Oh, of course, she said. Anything.

What was it like to have to take on that surrogate parent role so young?

Honestly, you brought me a lot of joy, and a sense of purpose. It was hard work, of course, and I sacrificed a more traditional adolescence, but it confirmed for me that I was meant to be a mother. The only time I felt overwhelmed was when you were figuring out your sexuality, she added tentatively.

We laughed awkwardly.

That was a weird time for everyone, yes, I said. I watched my face redden in the rearview mirror.

I didn't want to impose, nor did I want to wholly ignore

it, Donna continued. All I knew was that I had to love you unconditionally. I hope I did good.

You did better than anyone else could've, I said. I don't think I can thank you enough for that.

Watching those movies with you taught me a lot about love, so we both benefited, she said. I recited so many plagiarized romantic lines to Kent when we were dating. At that point, you were old enough to look out for yourself, so I was working at the grocery store. He asked me out at my till one day, took me to the beach that weekend, and before my next shift we'd agreed to date. It happened effortlessly, really: we moved into his parents' basement, then we bought a house on an acreage he'd been saving for since before we met. I decided I'd love him for as long as possible when he constructed me a garden and told me he wanted us to grow things together. And I never felt that my race was a problem for him, as it had been for other guys. He loved me for who I was, was never scared of anyone on the rez, though he probably should've been! Sometimes I'll look at him playing with the kids or making dinner or undressing and my heart will race as much as it did in those early days. The kids say they'll never leave, and part of me hopes they won't. But their dad and I will always be where they grew up. They'll always have a place to come back to, even when Kent and I are old and wrinkly and no longer making love. I'm so happy I can give that sort of permanency to them.

Auntie, that's literally so lovely. This call has been so, so helpful. You really, truly protected me. Your kids are lucky that you're their mom.

Through stifled crying, Donna said: You've always known how to make me cry. They'll be back anytime now, so we better stop this! We have supper plans and I don't want to reapply my makeup. Call me anytime! I have some sexier stories I can tell you. Love you.

I think I'll be okay in that department! I said, then ended the call, but not before luxuriating in our shared laughter.

•

The late summer sun was already quite low in the sky as I continued driving. It was red, like an apple.

I was a red man.

My longing was red.

My heart was a ripe fruit.

7

NO TRESPASSING

An almost animalistic instinct compelled me to turn off the highway and into a predominantly white hamlet named after a French Catholic priest from the early twentieth century. I wanted, for the first time as an adult, to return to the site of the Indian residential school my relatives were forced to attend as children. It was one of dozens in Alberta intended to brutalize rather than educate. This was an era of horror so prolonged and systematic that it continued to permeate the larger Indigenous consciousness. We were still haunted by it.

I stood in front of what was left of the residential school: a white entryway (chipped paint), the year 1947 etched into the entryway, a dark and empty room (to the extent I could know it was empty). Throughout adolescence I heard stories of supernatural disturbances spun from these remains: twirling figures, inexplicable sounds. Usually these were seen or heard during teen parties thrown in the hidden valley in which the abandoned school is situated, a graveyard just steps away. I never attended one, but almost everyone I knew had; it was somewhat of a rite of passage to do so, to barrel down the hill from a car or quad parked on the public side of a farmer's NO TRESPASSING sign. On this day, I was alone. The sky was vast and the grass was long and wild and in it my boots disappeared. Inside me: Nausea, the bitterness of the past. Also, a sense of how what I saw agitated representation. I wanted to take a photo and call it *The Unwritability of Grief*. I felt that I too could be photographed and labeled this way.

As a child, I knew little about the site; it was where I was brought to toboggan during winters. No one told me about the sick experiment that unfolded there, though later I would be told in a few words that a number of relatives had been forced to go there as children. It was this unspeakable fact that compelled me to return, though I now felt rebuked by it. The forest, the ground, these both seemed tinged with a sorrow older than I would ever be. The landscape was something I felt hurled at even as I was standing still.

What wasn't included in the public memory of a place was of deep ethical significance. The small community existed in a state of unremembering. Whenever I visited I felt like a ghost. An integral part of my personhood was unrecognizable. I was like the wind: noticeable only when I made something rustle.

As I stood, the sunlight crashed against me. I thought about what it would look like to practice a way of life that didn't amount to something like a Ministry of Historical Ignorance or a squad of memory police. At the very least, I wanted to erect a plaque that said:

HERE UNFOLDED CRIMES AGAINST INDIGE- NOUS CHILDREN IN THE NAME OF THE NATION.

HERE IS THE UNSTABLE GROUND OF TWENTY- FIRST CENTURY HAPPINESS AND MISERY.

I was reaching for a wildflower when from atop the hill a middle-aged white woman addressed me in an accusatory register: Excuse me, what are you doing?

I was caught off guard and couldn't respond with haste.

This isn't public property, she continued. A lot of us pay a lot of money to camp here, so if you aren't here to visit some- one, I think you should leave.

I pointed at the old school: You mean to say this is private property? Do you even know what it was?

She was meters away, but from where I stood I could see her face redden.

Some abandoned shed, I don't know, she said. That's beside the point. She inched backward. It seemed she was afraid of me.

I'm not trying to start anything, I said, knowing fully that I was plotted inside a semiotics of racism I wouldn't easily escape from. This was a residential school. I came here to mourn.

She paused, looked at the doorway. Then, as if refusing to solidify any sense of mutual understanding, she said: How do I know you're telling the truth?

Listen, I haven't given you a reason to distrust me, I responded. If you don't believe me, well . . .

Okay, it sounds like you're trying to make this about something it's not, she barked back. She reached for her phone from her back pocket, as if with it she could defend herself. She went on: I've never seen you before; you know what people are like. Where are you even from?

Her body, I supposed, betrayed her wish to not be seen as hostile or emotional. I saw her hands shaking, heard her voice break. She gestured in a circle, at the lake in the distance, at the forest, even. All this is campground, she said. The houses are back there, nowhere near here. You shouldn't have even driven onto the grass. She pointed at her feet. That's disrespectful, you know? There are already dirty ruts. I don't drive onto your backyard with my vehicle, she added.

I was astonished by her resolve to implicate me in affronts I hadn't made, to put blame, however ambiguous, onto me so as to absolve herself of any kind of wrongdoing. It was becoming clear she wanted to pull me into a battle I could only lose, because the world, this small pocket of it, at the end of the day, was hers to claim against political reason. What was also clear was that this kind of defense of property, even that which didn't legally belong to anyone, was bound up with the larger culture of amnesia that made it so a white woman could come upon a Cree man standing in front of what's left of a residential school and think she was in danger.

I'm not sure what to say, ma'am, I said. My relatives suffered here. My ancestors have lived on this lake for centuries. It is entirely within my right to be here. I was looking directly at her. I said this even though I knew it would sound to her like another dialect, if not an entirely different language.

I'm sorry, but I'm going to have to report you for trespassing. I'm done talking, she said. She put her phone to her ear. I knew she was calling the police. I also knew I couldn't reach my vehicle without walking within arm's reach, something neither of us wanted. So I walked into the forest, away from her, until her voice was drowned out by the density of trees. Was I evading the law? No, because I hadn't committed a crime. Yes, because the law in this country has always functioned as a suppresser of Indigenous life. To be Cree and alive, one had, in both minor and major ways, to evade the law, to stay out of its crosshairs. This woman wanted to make me into a moving target. The history that obscured the terror of the abandoned school was the same history that deputized her, that imbued her with a degree of legal power I didn't have, nor could I ever attain it if I wanted to. I didn't want to live like a weapon.

I would come back for my vehicle in an hour or so. I would come back to the site as well; in the fall, when the campers would have returned to their ends of the country. In the meantime, I decided, I will continue to live believing the story of Indigenous revolution has no ending, believing there will be nowhere that isn't already ours into which someone might think I was trespassing.

Eventually I arrived at the water. I walked past the

marina, crowded with boats and tourists, so as to reach a more secluded stretch of shoreline. The problem of private property arose once more; I wasn't sure who owned the patch of land upon which I was walking. I knew that no one could truly own the land and this thought emboldened me to stay put. The water was crashing gently at my feet. I was surprised at how opaque the lake was, how overtaken it was by algae, the kind that kept swimmers at bay. From where I stood, I could see the northwest edge of the lake, near which was another small community, this one named after a Catholic bishop. A residential school had also been located there, and I'd heard stories of Indigenous kids from farther south than Edmonton being transported like prisoners to this part of the province. I seldom cared to think about the concept of a soul, but I found myself thinking about it as I stared at the horizon, water extending in every direction. Could a place have a soul? If so, what kind of damage would all those decades of child abductions have done to the soul of these communities, to those who benefited from these acts of genocide? It pained me to think about it any further.

A MEMORY

All week I'd been trying to remember someone who was still alive. To die was to recede from the present, so, in a way, I thought, Jack had been living out a kind of social death. I wanted there to be a word for when history dictated that we stand in the middle of paradox like a doorway and not budge. Today, language was the sky falling onto me. Language was also something that hadn't been invented yet.

•

The summer Jack and I were thirteen, we both worked on the rez as seasonal student laborers. Mostly we mowed grass, added new coats of paint to various buildings, and helped with construction projects. It was the only economic opportunity available to us. After one shift, a number of us decided to drive our quads into the forest to hang out at a secluded stretch of river, as close to a private oasis as we could get. What was most important about the river was that it somehow felt untouched by the world. For a few hours, we lived in the magnificence of this feeling. As Indigenous youth, we were experts at doing so. We slept in the sun and played volleyball on the sandy embankment and Jack and one of our coworkers made out in the water and we let the unboundedness of their passion free us a little. Eventually the others left and it was just Jack and me amid the trembling poplars. Without prompt, he said, You know, I don't think I'll ever leave here. I don't think there's anywhere nearly this beautiful.

INTERLUDE

HEGEMONY

I returned to my hotel room determined to write, but nothing happened. I remembered reading Auden, who said that poetry makes nothing happen. I felt like the poets in this regard, insofar as I wanted my future novel to be like a "valley of its making"—to not be seen as someone trespassing onto already stolen land.

•

I opened Grindr and saw that Graham was hundreds of kilometers away, and so I measured my loneliness in kilometers; it
was an experience of distance.

I walked over to the A&W across the parking lot to buy
a burger. The walls were plastered in black-and-white photographs of older versions of the restaurant. It made me pause,
because what was nostalgia if not a kind of hunger?

•

My phone buzzed with a Facebook message:

River: *what's fieldwork called when it's for a novel?*
Me: *group therapy?*
River: *LOL*
River: *so, the trip's been . . . a lot??*
Me: *i'm not entirely certain i know what i'm doing
anymore, but i believe there's a story here,
about how people are made to participate in
the production of their own misery.*
Me: *i guess that's the definition of hegemony, isn't
it? Lmao*
River: *yes, i do believe it is haha*
River: *but just because an experience has definitional
clarity doesn't mean it's thoroughly
understood or represented. what it feels like*

to exist under that kind of pressure is so
circumstantial. it is our job to translate our
individual language of suffering.

•

I combed through my copy of Barthes's *Mourning Diary*. One of the sentences I underlined twice: "Mourning: a cruel country where I am no longer afraid." For the colonized, the same could be said of the future, of one's own body.

All language is raw and improvised, I thought, shot out of an unrehearsed mouth. It took me years to accept this. In my hotel room I decided that I didn't want to conceal my fluttering body anymore. My future sentences would ache.

I picked up my notebook and wrote: *Can one write like a community? Where the narrative voice isn't individual but plural? Is this the first-person plural?*

8

SMALL TERRORS

I read a Facebook post from an old friend detailing an abusive relationship she'd just exited. Her name was Robin, and she'd been dating a man named Mark. Mark wasn't one of our peers because he had graduated years before us; rather, he was the kind of man who lingered around teenagers, didn't move on from high school. He was big, imposing. He exuded a subtle mischievousness, and so he wasn't someone I could ever fathom trusting. *At first*, Robin wrote, *I felt protected by him. Until I didn't.* She had just ended the turbulent relationship and had taken to social media, she explained, because she didn't want to remain silent. She wanted to warn others about the harm he inflicted and likely would continue to inflict. *We have to hold these kinds of men accountable*, she concluded. It was a call to action, and an act of prayer. There were comments upon comments from other women saying, *I believe you* and *fuck that guy* and *I hope you press charges!*

There are so many stories of this sort about these kinds of men, I thought. Men who backed people into the corners of their lives, who set everything ablaze, who walked toward the fire and put their hands to it. These men demanded a certain formlessness from women, demanded that they exist as containers for their anguish. In other words, they wanted to reign over meaning, to force the genre of women to engender the same thing without end: the end of women.

To write out of northern Alberta I had to do so in a feminist mode, I thought. I needed to insist on a form of gender that wasn't a natural disaster but rather a sprawling field where nothing was a coffin someone could fall into.

I wrote to Robin: *hey, I'm in town, it's been ages, are you free for a walk?*

Mark got a job up north about a year and a half into the relationship, Robin said.

We were walking along a side road that bypassed the main street. To our left was a train track and beyond that was an expanse of farmers' fields. Robin looked as she had when we were in high school together, youthful and warm.

Her consideration felt unconditional, democratic. This made her willingness to join me on an impromptu walk less surprising. She was dressed in an oversized flannel shirt and jean shorts. We laughed when we first approached each other, as I was essentially wearing the same outfit. I felt immediately at ease with her despite not having kept in touch during the intermediate years.

At first it was a blessing, she said. He'd been unemployed for months after getting let go from the mill when it announced an imminent closure. I was only working part-time at the grocery store because I was taking some courses at the college. His great-uncle, or something like that, got him an interview. The next week he flew to a camp near Fort McMurray, started working as a junior mechanic under the supervision of his great-uncle. It was shift work, seven days on, four days off. It was hard for me to adjust to the rhythm, having already lived with him for a year, having spent every day with him during that time. His absence, which was more accurately the absence of his chaos, startled me. He brought a lot of noise into my life. He generally spoke loudly and was always ranting about something, usually something problematic. I often ignored him, she continued, which didn't bother him. He didn't want me to engage anyway, he only wanted to be heard.

A matter of receptivity, I thought. The fact of being vulnerable to another's language, regardless of if we respond or not.

Whenever he wasn't working, she continued, we talked on the phone for hours during those first few weeks. When he came home, there was so much passion between us. The time apart rekindled something in our relationship that I didn't realize had been disintegrating. He was newly tender. I fell in love with him all over again. As she said this, a train's horn blared in the distance. I almost didn't hear her.

That feeling of bliss was short-lived, of course, she added. One day, after the typical six-hour drive, he arrived home angry. He said that a bunch of his coworkers had been laid off, including the one guy he'd gotten closest with. Everyone was blaming the New Democratic Party government, saying they were endangering everyone's way of life, the Albertan way. He was swearing and shouting offensive words so loudly the neighbors called the next day to ask if I was okay. I was so embarrassed. When we first met I didn't yet have the vocabulary to understand the kind of person he was, but I was taking introductory courses in sociology and political science and the instructors really changed how I saw the world. Mark was a large straight white man whose family literally helped settle this region. And yet here he was decrying the end of some era of Albertan dominance or whatever. It's fucked up.

With this remark, I felt seen in a way I hadn't all week. Her structural analysis, however terse, reminded me that my academic training enabled me to see in a way that my rural upbringing hadn't. We saw what we saw in the same light. In this was a kind of intimacy.

In the wake of that moment, Robin said, I started to rethink the relationship, to revisit the past and assess his actions differently. As I said, he brought a lot of turbulence into my life, and it was so persistent and normalized I became numb to it.

He was constantly accusing me of infidelity and disliked my parents so much he talked me out of visiting them on numerous occasions. My family, as you know, is almost accidentally liberal, as well as firmly middle class. He felt like an outsider, coming from a working-class family. He never contributed to conversation. He carried a great deal of shame about the poverty he grew up in. When he was out of work, he spiraled into a depression. It challenged his sense of his own manhood. He felt that he wasn't providing for us, especially since I'd taken over paying most of the bills. To him, this was a deep moral failing. During that period, I found myself worrying that he would resort to violence, though I somehow rationalized that possibility as unexceptional, as something men inflicted on their loved ones all the time.

I watched him from a distance after that, she continued. I would notice the small terrors he brought into my life, but I was unable to confront him about them. Every time he returned from the oil field he had a new story about how radical leftists and whatnot were ruining the province, the country. He even started saying homophobic shit about one of our oldest friends, someone he once respected. It pulled me out of whatever fantasy I had about the man he could become, the man my love could transform him into. As I was preparing myself to break up with him, coordinating with my parents and cousins about a getaway strategy, he did what I described in my Facebook post. For the most part, I avoided having discussions with him about the upcoming election. I had no reason to believe he'd participate in an open discussion about our political beliefs and how they differed. On election day, he had to travel back to the camp and would vote before leaving town. As he was heading out of the door, he called me over and told me to give him a kiss, which was pretty routine. Then he pulled me closer to his chest, and the next thing I know I'm in a headlock, gasping for air. He whispered into my ear that I had to vote for the conservative candidate or he'd fuck me up. Then he laughed, he fucking laughed in my face, as I was crying.

I voted that afternoon because he wanted me to take a photograph outside the polling station. I went to the poll, but I spoiled the ballot. My vote wouldn't have mattered in the grand scheme of things, especially so in northern Alberta, the conservative stronghold that it is, but he wanted to dictate it in order to begin to control me. He knew that I wasn't just voting against his preferred candidate, but against the person he had become.

Do you think he realized he'd become radicalized? I asked.

I don't, she said. He felt owed a particular degree of wealth and social capital for no reason other than who he was and the history he was connected to. So I left. I stopped answering his calls and texts and moved out of the house. He parked outside of my parents' house for a few days, even smashed their headlights. But then he moved on. I heard he was seeing another girl the next week. My Facebook post was partly a signal to her. I hope she sees it.

As for me, she went on, I feel free.

I was reminded of my own experience of freeing myself from the looming threat of toxic masculinity. Emotional unavailability and domination were the two primary modes available to me; the men around me rarely deviated from those scripts. A boy stepped into one or both of them the way one stepped into a house, with a kind of quiet triumph. But I was predisposed to another way of being, one rooted in joy and care, one that didn't bulldoze those around me. Robin was right, I thought, one had to pursue what was otherwise. The result was indeed a kind of freedom.

Next month, she continued, I will move to Edmonton to start a degree in education. I want to come back and teach teenagers, maybe empower kids who were like us, kids who needed glimpses of the world beyond this boreal forest. As she said this she gestured toward the trees that lined the horizon.

What's your book about, by the way? Robin asked.

I told her I couldn't satisfyingly answer the question, which was and wasn't a lie, something close enough to the truth. At this half explanation she shook her head.

If anything, I ad-libbed, not wanting to appear secretive or pretentious, I intend it to show that the disregarded sometimes live the most remarkable lives, but there's so much we have to unsee to see that in its entirety. I hope I know how to.

As I said this Robin grabbed my hand and squeezed it. You do, she said, you do.

9

A HISTORY OF FREEDOM

After stowing my bags away, I composed a two-part tweet from my vehicle in the hotel parking lot: *My theory of aesthetics is that if you're queer you're predisposed to the condition of overwriting because when you come into your identity after a time of closetedness excess becomes a way of plotting yourself in a different story than the one you inherited. It's literally gay to be a bad writer!* I hit send, then drove off. The tweets received four likes in twenty minutes.

Twenty minutes from town meant I was arriving in the

rez to which I politically belonged. It was the first day of the annual powwow and I had arranged to meet my cousin Lena there before I made the drive south. Her daughter was competing in the children's jingle dress category for the first time, and I was tearful at the thought of seeing her.

Reserves like mine are full of visual irony and metaphor, I thought, though few expend the analytical energy to understand them as such. Highway 2, part of the Trans-Canada Highway, the skeleton of the nation, bifurcates the community, splitting it in half. Droves of vehicles traverse the highway day after day, witness firsthand that those on the rez live lives with no singular emotional arc, but outsiders still refuse to break their ties to the racist optic that denies us complexity. They see what they want, what they've been empowered to see. My rez, like most in Canada, came into being so as to function like an open-air prison, but today, against this logic, we care for one another in ways that the state could and will never interrupt.

As I drove past the police detachment, a recent addition, I noticed that in the ditch four kids—preteens—were walking with two dogs of indiscernible breeds at their side. They'd been laughing; one of them was hanging on to another's shoulder, his hand at his chest. The third was shaking his head, and the fourth was wiping a tear from her eye. Their joy was radiant. Even I, encased in steel, moving at an eighty-kilometer-an-hour pace, felt awash in it. They were the happiest people I'd seen in a very long time.

From the highway, the heart of the rez unfolded before me: the band office and social services building on the right, the skating rink and community center and baseball fields on the left, houses surrounding everything. I glanced judiciously at where my grandparents and cousins lived, tried to catch a glimpse of their goings-on, as I always did, but I was moving too fast. I spent significant parts of my childhood here, so much so that for many years I didn't distinguish between it and the town where my mom had moved after she finished high school, the town in which I grew up. I remember thinking I could walk down the street from my front door and wind up at a relative's house. My world was small, but I had no idea of scale and no use for it. For all I knew, this was where I would live and die.

Amid this sudden bout of nostalgia, I wondered whether I should have done my research on the rez, endeavored to write a novel about those who have a long history of refusing to let their surroundings usurp their agency. Perhaps I should have given more discursive space to the stories of those like Mary. But then I reminded myself that I had no plans other than to write things down, which is to say I had time to write three versions of this novel and I would still have plenty of room for human pleasure and displeasure.

The powwow was one of many on the North American circuit. I'd heard stories of dancers traveling from one prairie province to the next all summer, going back and forth, ignorant of the borders that divided them, those divisions no longer practical, if they ever were. The powwow, held over three days, had a gravitational pull, its own rhythms and norms; when I was a kid, it always felt as if I were stepping into something wondrous, another world. This feeling struck me again as I parked among the rows and rows of vehicles and tents and RVs that had already settled into the space. Everything adhered to a circular structure: The core was the grass on which the dancers danced. Layered around that was the arbor, public seating. From there unraveled a layer for folks to walk around, another for vendors to sell art and crafts and food, another for the vehicles and campers. From some angles, it looked like a planet. From others, a beating heart.

Cell service was spotty, as often happened when so many people congregated on the grounds, but a text from Lena came through nonetheless; she informed me she was seated near a flag emblazoned with the logo of the regional tribal council. Lena was considerably older than me, but she had always been a dear confidante. After I'd gotten my driver's license, I stayed at her house now and then. She'd just met the future father of her children, so usually I was a third wheel or was left to my own devices, neither of which I resented. I was practicing how to be autonomous, how to be someone outside the limits of my childhood home. I thus made it a habit of stopping by her place whenever I was in the area.

I cut through the crowd walking clockwise around the arbor. I thought of the many hours my cousins and I, including Jack and Lena, walked around and around and around in an endless circle without growing bored. It was enough to be part of something thrumming and alive.

Lena stood up as I approached the wooden bleachers. She

was wearing a form-fitting tracksuit, though it would soon be too hot to be in head-to-toe polyester. I don't think she particularly cared about the heat; what mattered most was that she looked beautiful. Her hair was in a topknot and from her ears swayed bold neon earrings made by an Indigenous designer whose tweets had recently gone viral. Beneath her was a blanket she'd laid out for her and her kids to sit on. A strip of 50/50 tickets dangled from her hand.

Ah my god, it's good to see you, my handsome cousin, she said, pulling me into an embrace. The kids have been asking about you. They're running around, but they'll be happy you're here.

I sat down beside her. The bleachers were already full; from a cursory glance, I saw too many familiar faces to count. I hadn't been to the powwow since my first degree; I felt a pang of regret. It seemed I had missed so much.

So, my love, what's new? Lena said. Tell me about the Ph.D. Are you already turning it into a book?

Well, I stammered, I'm putting the Ph.D. on hold right now. It was loosely about grief as a critical position, as a way of making claim to the world.

Like that film you suggested we watch? The one about the trail in Saskatchewan, Lena said. We did watch it. I cried at the ending, at the beautiful animation. It reminded me of a eulogy, like I was being asked to mourn with the filmmaker. It was powerful to see the truth so clearly depicted. I never thought I'd see something like it in my lifetime. As she said this, her voice broke.

I don't want to cry right now, Lena interjected. Not at the powwow while the emcee is telling his usual dad jokes. She laughed boisterously.

That experience of collective lament was exactly what I was thinking about, I added. I suppose I still am.

This is a different project? Lena asked. How have the interviews gone? How's Mary? You spoke with her earlier this week, I heard. Rez gossip. She nudged my shoulder.

She's going through so much, with Jack being in jail, I said. She loves him deeply. I could feel it in the air. She's been defending his life. I keep trying to figure out how to describe the depth of her care, and I think "defense" is the closest I'll get. It's profound, really. But also heartbreaking, of course. I've been thinking about her all week.

I've been meaning to visit her more, Lena said. I'm sure she'd love to see the kids. She has such a big yard; we could fit most of the family there. I see her now and then at the health center or the store or the bingo hall. She always gives me a big hug, calls me her girl. I think everyone sympathizes with her struggle. We all think about her.

I was struck, though I didn't mention it, by this "we," a pronoun as vast and emotional as history. Lena, on account of having been on the rez her whole life, could marshal this collective voice. She was one of many in a chorus that sang of flourishing and grief.

As for the book, I said, I haven't written anything yet. There's so much language inside me. I feel like I'm going to explode with it, like light. But I don't have the urge to write. This is a new sensation for me. I'm worried it means I won't be able to bring the novel to life, that maybe it can't be a novel, that there's too much at stake.

I don't know much about publishing, Lena said, but maybe that feeling means you *have* to write it.

Maybe you're right, I said. What seems to be resonant with everyone I interviewed is the belief that we have to tell our stories, that storytelling will redeem us somehow, make us less lonely.

Mhmm, especially so for natives. If any native recorded the circumstances of her life, from childhood to old age, it'd be a better novel than anything those white guys write about.

We laughed. An auntie leaned toward us as if to partake in the merriment.

Enough about me, I said after a pause. How're the kids doing?

They're both so amazing, cuz, I sometimes can't believe it. I'm doing my best to make sure they have chances to learn about their culture. My girl is competing for the first time, hopefully the first of many powwows. When I watch her I just sob. It's as if she is magical, untouchable. Those little bells warm my heart so much. My boy might take after you, I think. She nudged me with her elbow. We watch that drag show together, she continued. I sometimes see him watching me, analyzing me for little clues as to whether or not I'll accept him. I will, of course. I've been using their slang: *Yes god!* We laughed again.

He's so sensitive to the world, feels so much. He asked to be put in ballet in the fall, and of course I said yes. I protect them. I give them space to think and exist, something I never had. They're my best friends. I can't wait to see what they accomplish. I want the world for them. I don't want them to have to fight like we did, Lena said.

Earlier I'd spotted her boy among a group of preteens. He did indeed have an air of femininity to him, though it was subtle, as mine was when I was his age. Sexuality was something other people had, a place others visited, though many thrust the label onto me all the same. This drive to identify my nonnormativity always confused me. Because I was consumed by hobbies and school, I wasn't thinking about whom or what I desired. For a while, I was squished inside an identity others imagined for me based on fear and stereotypes. As an adult, I had to dig myself out of myself, had to make myself into a ruin from which something new could grow. I hoped Lena's boy wouldn't have to go through the same existential struggle. Perhaps instead he would come of age fully grounded in his queerness, wouldn't feel the urgency to repress it the way I did. Times were changing, however slowly. After all, Lena was the kind of mother who, like Donna, like Mary, would architect a world with whatever materials were available in which their children's joy could be infinite.

Hey, Lena said, I've been meaning to ask you something.

Yes, please, I said, almost hungrily.

Her demeanor shape-shifted, became more serious. You know, she said, you haven't come around much since you first left for university. Why's that?

I was taken aback, but only partly so, because it was a question that had hung over plenty of the conversations I'd had with relatives whenever I visited. Their silent pleas sometimes said: *What did we do? What didn't we do?* Now I understood it was a kind of cruelty to allow these questions to go unanswered, to let them loom over everything like bad weather.

Oof, that's a doozy, I said, then chuckled nervously. Where to begin? Well, I remember how strong my desire to leave was when I was in high school, when I realized I wouldn't be able to live openly as a queer person here, wouldn't be able to love and be loved in the way I wanted. My yearning dominated me, really. It led me to thinking sex was the main way I could demonstrate my queerness. I had to figure everything out alone. The first time I went to the STI clinic was one of the scariest moments of my life. I had to acquire a new language, get schooled in new codes of being. Maybe a part of me resented where I'd come from, because I felt so behind, so foreign. And then when these feelings receded, it was too late, I had moved on. Lena put her hand over mine, moved closer to me. But, I went on, I don't want that to be the way things are anymore. Wanting to write a novel about northern Alberta might in part be my way of initiating some sort of homecoming. In interviewing everyone, it's like I've accessed a self-knowledge I had lost sight of.

Lena looked me squarely in the eyes. We can't wait to have you back, dear.

Just then the emcee cut through the chatter of the seated crowd to announce that the youngest jingle dress dancers would soon be called forth. Lena screamed and gave me a kiss on the cheek. That's my cue, she said. I need to go wrangle my daughter. Can you watch my things? I'll be back. I said yes, of course, but she'd already darted toward the roving children.

Lena's daughter's regalia was handmade by a local elder and seamstress. The bells fell down her tiny body like a waterfall. The dress itself was a vibrant pink, nearly identical to the shade of her mother's outfit. Standing together, they looked like versions of the same person at different points in a single life. It felt to me like a poem. The daughter planted herself near the middle of the grassy field. As the drummers sang, as the sounds vibrated through us, I couldn't help but watch Lena, how affected she was by her daughter's gentle movements, by this scene of cultural expression. A whole history of freedom was unfolding before me. It was so magnificent I hoped I'd see it again and again.

A MEMORY

The summer before I moved to Edmonton, Jack interviewed for a job with a construction company. He had to pass a drug test as part of the process. He wouldn't pass, even if he'd stopped smoking weed when he first got wind of the opening. He'd known of a friend storing someone else's urine in a temperature-regulated pouch hidden in his pants without getting caught. So he texted me out of the blue to ask if I could pee in a bottle for him. I was the only person he knew around our age who didn't do drugs. I said yes; I was already politically astute enough to oppose drug screening in the workplace. When he retrieved the urine, Jack said to me, I owe you, man. The few

times I saw him in the subsequent years, he always repeated
the phrase, though he didn't refer back to the favor. During the
few weeks that he stayed at my apartment, he often thanked
me. One night when I picked him up after a late shift, he said,
No one's really looking out for me, man. What you're doing, it
means a lot to me. Before I could respond, he'd already closed
his eyes, his breathing had already slowed.

10

HIGHWAY 2

About an hour east of the rez, I noticed a political placard affixed to a stop sign at a nondescript intersection. This was out of the ordinary because the provincial election had ended months ago, in the spring, and this particular candidate—a middle-aged white man, a new member of the Conservative Party—had secured his spot in the legislature in Edmonton. I remembered hearing about a bylaw that penalized candidates who failed to remove the placards the day after the election. It didn't surprise me that this small refutation of the law endured; to many it likely constituted a kind of show-boating. The placard transformed the stop sign into a flag, heroically planted in a land so many voters felt bound to, felt was theirs to own, despite an enduring Indigenous presence. Already the ruling party had implemented austerity measures the only survivors of which would be the upper classes. Secondary school curriculum was being demodernized, teachers and nurses were being fired, health care was being privatized, amenities and resources were being deregulated, climate change was being accelerated. From the outside, from a leftist standpoint, it appeared as if it were a marker of political action to endorse the cheapening of one's quality of life, that it was normal and a generational birthright to vote on the side of structurally induced hardship. Perhaps some wanted to conjure a scapegoat, something (a government) and someone (a politician) to blame when one's individual or familial struggles to live a good life fell short, acting on a suspicion that the game was rigged against them, though a culture of anti-intellectualism would prevent them from diagnosing why. A punishing government was a burden they could choose, one that would keep them from installing too much optimism in what a future could reap. From year to year things changed very little, one's threats to existence remained the same, and so liveliness coalesced as the negation of change, of difference. A common enemy, in other words, is another name for social cohesion.

The Conservative base was being held together by always-intensifying emotions, by heteropatriarchal feelings of possessorship and nativism in particular that found expression as rage and self-pity. The former was regularly aimed at others, the non-normative, namely queers and immigrants, who were coded as squatters on the private property of the everyday. Rather than ameliorate their state of loss, rather than build a political system that by definition would democratize institutional care, conservatives chose again and again to live in a dead world, one that was programmed only to amplify its deadness. It seemed to me that their dogma could be summarized like this: *If we're all subject to planetary catastrophe, if we experience the same intensity of existential fragility as the downtrodden, let us descend into madness and disaster, but we will govern the pace!* What a brutal legacy to be a recipient of by virtue of geographic fate, I thought. It's a miracle anyone escapes it.

I stopped at the first roadside truck stop in more than a hundred kilometers. Unthinkingly, I opened the Grindr app, which revealed a grid of mostly ghost profiles, some with no information whatsoever, others with just an age or height. A minority went against the grain and posted pictures of their faces, the names of their small towns glowing in the surrounding blackness, as if neon signs. What was and wasn't brave in the world of the sexual changed drastically the farther one traveled from an urban center. I wished there were a way to communicate the equivalent of a non-sexual salute, something to show I recognized the social cost they paid and would continue to pay, a gesture of solidarity. A similar bewilderment welled inside me while I glanced down at my phone as when I sat across from Michael in his apartment. How does one make do with so little? Does it feel as though one still has to defend a secret, that one's entire being vibrates with it? Or was I thinking of the state of their lives improperly? Did rurality constitute a kind of defense against the vulnerability of outness and, therefore, of love? Did the interiority of their sexuality make their senses of selfhood feel more legible, rigid? What would my Grindr brethren make of this sort of line of thinking? Did the app make them feel part of a country, allegiant to the same values of lust and self-fabrication, singers of the same anthem of risk and longing? I knew it would have been disingenuous, offensive even, to articulate this in a chat, for these were men who were hoping to score a date or a fast orgasm or at the very least a digital companion, none of which I could provide, so I said nothing and exited the app. Already I'd received a handful of messages and two dick pics.

As I pumped gas into my vehicle an older white man pulled up behind me in a truck with years of rust above the tires. As he jumped down, the thud his boots made disturbed the seriousness I'd brought to the task of refueling, of lamenting the hypothetical unhappiness of rural gay men in twenty-first century Alberta. Our gazes, similarly curious, analytical, locked, then fell away. His was a simple portrait to paint: He looked like dozens of other men of his age, race, and location, all of whom, in my mind, were as clad in faded denim as he was. Resultantly, I boxed him in a stereotype, so much so that I was momentarily worried he was going to call me a faggot or something else resonant with the fury of prejudice. To my surprise and alarm he put the nozzle back into the pump, then approached me.

Excuse me, he said cautiously, his palms hoisted before me, as if I were a possibly rabid animal he was attempting to soothe. I don't mean to intrude, but I wanted to thank you.

I laughed, louder and heartier than I would have liked, as it suggested ease.

My son came out to us last year, he continued, perhaps encouraged by my laughter. I shouldn't assume, but . . . I nodded. (Was it the short shorts? The septum piercing? My general demeanor? Everything about me?) It was hard for everyone, he went on. We didn't know what to say for a long time, for weeks, which hurt him, of course.

I wanted to tell him that his son likely spent every morning inside that silence reinventing the concept of joy, that his hands were likely very callused because of it, but I couldn't. I couldn't muster up the bravery he did to briefly puncture the social contract of affective distance that strangers cosign. How suddenly a boy can transform from a loved one to an unknowable music, I thought.

The old man readjusted his hat. He's our only child, he continued. We thought we'd done something wrong, that we were being punished. And we were worried for him, are worried for him, we know what this world is like. I said so many terrible things throughout his childhood, I was sure he hated me. His voice waned, became atonal, precious, as if prone to shattering.

The other day, he told me, it occurred to him that the anger he directed at his son was, in actuality, anger at himself, for failing to open up space for his son to experiment and make mistakes and challenge the adults around him. He'd been so totalitarian. In a moment of something like confession he shook his head, as if to rebuke the flood of emotion and, with it, his culpability. He was glad to see others like his son around here, he summarized. I couldn't tell him I was simply passing through, that this was a place in which I could only ever briefly exist. I couldn't spoil the fantasy that I was, somehow, his son, that he finally said what he needed to say. But, in the end, he would still need to speak with his own child.

He extended his hand out to me, which I shook firmly. I felt an unexpected sense of pride, as if I were actually a kind of rarely sighted hero, as if I were indeed miraculous enough to be worthy of his praise.

I had almost forgotten that all my experiences added up to a normal life. I realized I had pitied the old man and he had likely pitied me too, that this shared pity enabled us to converse in the first place—it was our common idiom. Perhaps this had been the case with all my interviewees; perhaps this is the case with human sociality generally. Humans are pitiable because we are unfree from the scripts inside another's head; but we rebel. Was I endeavoring to hear the sounds made when someone broke through a story they hadn't written for themselves? At that moment I couldn't think of anything else worth doing.

•

As I approached Edmonton, a deer lay dead on the shoulder of the highway, heavily stained with its blood. Crows danced around the carcass as I drove by. It was a scene so common I initially thought nothing of it. Then, suddenly, I was plummeted into a mindfulness that brought into focus the embargo on grief in which I was about to participate. What would it mean to stop everything and stand by the deer? To claim the loss as mine, at least partly? To rip the scene from ordinary life and imbue it with shock and an extravagant kind of sadness? What would that have done, made possible? Maybe nothing. It was already too late to find out. Minutes later, my grief was already a failure.

INTERLUDE

AUGUST

It was past eight in the evening when I got back to my apartment, though there was still plenty of light in the sky. I was nostalgic for the summer even though it hadn't yet surrendered to autumn. I felt that I couldn't waste the last days of August. Maybe I could still fall in love, I thought. I've always said that it'd still be August in my body when I died. Tonight this sentiment had roused me the way an anthem might. If I were to die prematurely, which was a statistical probability, I wanted to be in love as long as humanly possible.

What is a human possibility? I wondered. Love? I had few reasons to believe that that was the case, but I believed it all the same.

When I was growing up, everyone around me was in a relationship. Some of the couples in my family had been together for decades. No one was single, and if they were, they were treated with circumspection. Loneliness was a curse, something to be avoided at all costs. I've always felt desperate to be in love, even as a closeted teenager, especially as a closeted teenager. I've made all this racket about ideas and literature and art, but really what I've wanted most was to be loved. I was reminded of this hierarchy of desire when I was in bed with Graham. If even a stranger in a hotel room could seem like a greater counter to my existential malaise than anything else, then perhaps I was fated to want any activity, be it writing or thinking or reading or traveling, to be as intense and spellbinding as an experience of infatuation. This wasn't an easy way to live, I knew. Still, I had no idea how to live otherwise.

As I stepped into my kitchen, I saw the extent of how disheveled my life was with more clarity than ever. Books were strewn about everywhere. Dirty dishes piled up in the sink, dirty laundry spilling out of the bathroom. My fridge was empty save for expired eggs and milk. I'd externalized my inner turmoil, my state of academic crisis, my sadness. My initial thought was that I needed to relocate, to find a new place to live, but then that panic gave way to the realization that I couldn't live my life as if I were on the run all the time. Perhaps I fetishized love because it represented a stability I rarely had. A fetish is a fetish because of its aura of unattainability. What if part of me refused love as much as I ached for it? What if I wanted to destroy myself as much as I wanted to be saved?

I wasn't sure what exactly I could do with these questions, so I added my bags to the mess and sat solemnly on the couch. The air was stale, as I had forgotten to open a window before I left. The walls around me were bare; I never felt compelled to hang anything up, not even my degrees, not even family photos. I thought about turning on the TV, but there was nothing I wanted to watch. I thought about my mother again. I wondered how the barbecue had gone. I hadn't been inside her house in a long time, I realized. She had refurnished my childhood bedroom when I moved out, converted it into a guest room. I wasn't sentimental about my childhood, but I did think at the time that this was a strange decision. In a way, I'd been expunged from the space. Maybe it was necessary, a small way of reckoning with our uneasy relationship, putting it to rest or starting over. The memory didn't summon anger or sadness in me, as I too had tried to move on.

But I now understood that my forgiveness couldn't go unspoken. It wasn't a void we could live inside.

Into the stale apartment air, I said, Mom, I forgive you.

It wasn't sorrow I felt but peace. I would say these words to her directly, I would stand in front of her and forgive her. For the first time, this seemed inevitable. We didn't have to go into the particulars, I decided. She didn't have to respond at all, for that matter. Like August, the conversation would mark the fading away of one season and the promise of another. A mother's love—I needed to fight for and defend it as much as I would any of my political values. Perhaps making room for my mother's love, I thought, was a politics in and of itself.

11

TESTIMONY

I approached the Remand Centre in a state of disorientation. The parking lot was mostly vacant and yet I parked as far away from the main entrance as possible. I had no sense of protocol or social norm and so I was more nervous than I expected to be. My hands trembled and my eyes scanned everything around me rapidly and without focus. As I entered, I stumbled toward what I assumed was a reception desk. The lobby, though that word seemed wrong for a correctional facility, was small, as if few people actually ever ended up waiting in it. The sun was high in the sky, but its heat pervaded the space nonetheless. The guard stationed behind the desk looked at me with a kind of cruel curiosity. I found it hard to maintain eye contact with him; my eyes wandered to his bulletproof vest, then to the gun teetering at his waist.

After moments of awkward silence, he finally spoke: Place all your belongings, your cell phone, wallet, keys, whatever, in a locker. From behind a glass barrier, he gestured toward the entrance where a row of lockers stood. He tossed me a small key. I would have to give it back to him before moving through the metal detector, he instructed. The detector, I noted, would mark a transition of sorts into a more hypermediated realm where my entire body, my entire personhood, would be subject to interrogation, to surveillance from nowhere and everywhere. This sent a jolt a panic through me. As I emptied my pockets, I was struck by another realization: everything that made up the texture and mechanics of the prison—total control, alienation, an atmosphere of fear, the ever-present threat of violence—existed in the world outside it. In fact, the idea of an "outside" was untrue, misleading even. There were many kinds of legalized violence, practiced by people every day. There were many kinds of arenas for punishment and surveillance, and we lived inside them our whole lives. The prison was where all of these tactics and arenas existed in their most monstrous forms.

The guards watching from the other side of the metal detector looked at me—a stranger—not with skepticism but with what I thought was complete comprehension, or what they were empowered by history, by sociology and statistics, to know with bodily clarity. I was a coherent object inside a prison; my identity was narratively sound in it. I was a possible inmate. I shared an intimacy of proximity, both in terms of geography and culture, with those inside. We were all a part of a single manhunt.

As a guard patted my body, I could feel sweat thickening under my armpits.

It felt as if I were being led through a labyrinth, a door then another door then another. Finally, one of the doors opened onto what seemed to be the stomach of the prison. Its vastness—the wideness of the room, the height of the ceiling—suggested a sense of scale seemingly at odds with its practices of containment. At first I thought this paradox was a problem of form, that the prison inherently exposed the impossibility of its own project, that it couldn't hold everyone inside it, that the agents of state power couldn't detain everyone they sought to. It occurred to me instead that what mattered was the replicability of the space. Because racism and economic precarity continue to intensify rather than lessen, one prison necessitates another, then another. Little changes inside them; they reproduce the same structure of feeling, the same conditions of consciousness, the same engineered states of endangerment. The dimensions are less important than the fact of being detained.

I started to think, oddly enough, about how novels frame human existence and sensation so narrowly that a character can appear to be trapped in a structure without agency. This wasn't analogous to a prison by any means, but in my mind it seemed to underscore the way normal people, writers that is, play the part of a security guard or a correctional officer under the auspices of literature.

Everywhere that didn't hold inmates was adorned with reflective glass. The obvious function of this was to destroy the subject-object distinction, to make everyone into subject-objects of the carceral gaze. As I was led deeper into the prison all my powers of concentration went into the newly impossible task of not looking at myself, of looking away from myself. Were I to allow the mirrors to fix my attention, I thought, I wouldn't trust what I saw emulated back.

The mirrors also added to the "state-of-the-art" aesthetic of the prison, a description that nauseated upon my first encounter of it during a Google search.

The Remand Centre was Canada's largest prison, and, like other infrastructures of legally sanctioned cruelty, it relied on the visual to authorize the inhumanity practiced within its walls. This was immediately clear to me. Located just off the Anthony Henday, a superhighway that connects the north, south, east, and west parts of the city in a giant circle, the Remand Centre was a twenty-first century creation where a nineteenth and twentieth century hatred of Indigenous peoples ran rampant. It was built to allow for the imprisonment of as many as possible while also aiming to summon visual pleasure. The façade, the intricate internal corridors, the décor—every decision of style added up in my mind up to an architectural care that obfuscated the lack of state welfare and historical justice delivered to the mostly Indigenous population in the cells. It is all of our duty, I thought, to rebel against the beautification of violence. I recognized this straightaway as the raison d'être of the countercultural novel.

As I was struggling to avoid my reflection, I locked eyes with a guard stationed behind a desk at which a monitor displayed the hallway through which I was moving. What I sensed first was his contempt for me, an interloper, someone who cared for someone he punished. I troubled his fantasy of absolute punishment, humanized those he was paid to dehumanize. I was a sign of his guiltiness, something that made him alert to the blood on his hands. What I noticed second was that he looked like Mark, Robin's ex-boyfriend. In a sense, he was Mark, was the brutalizer Mark represented. Everything about him suggested a desire to brutalize, especially in a politically legitimized way, a way for which he would be lauded. In his sight line, I was a kind of prey. I shuddered. He saw this happen twice: on the screen and in real life.

•

Jack was seated behind a translucent barrier, which called to mind James Baldwin: "I hope that nobody has ever had to look at anybody they love through glass." He was wearing an orange jumpsuit, just like those in the many curiously popular TV series about prisons. The fabric looked cheap, uncomfortable. The jumpsuit contrasted the architectural flourishes inside and outside the center. To my mind, it demonstrated how much more prison was about hiding people away rather than it was about justice. I was surprised by how much Jack looked like me, though he was more muscular, as he had always been. His head had been shaved, which made his face look smaller and more vulnerable than I'd ever seen it. After we said our hellos, I told him I'd visited Mary. He seemed to choke up at the mention of her name. I asked if he wouldn't mind talking to me about how he'd ended up here. He said it was a long story. I told him we could start with his earliest memories. We had time, not much, but enough. He spoke uninterruptedly.

I'm standing with Kokum at the window of our house watching a bear and two cubs move through the yard. I'd been outside, playing on the porch, when Kokum pulled me inside. I hadn't seen the bears just up ahead. It's not fear that I remember but a feeling of comfort, safety. Kokum was my world. Everything I knew had to do with her. I could tell that she was shaken. She said, Don't leave my sight. All I said was, I won't. I meant it. Why would I?

I don't remember ever having to distinguish my kokum from my mom. Do you know what I mean? My mom, who would drop by now and then, she had less of a presence to me than Kokum, less, uh, importance. No one ever really asked me about my parents. People knew Mary was raising me. It wasn't uncommon. A lot of my childhood friends had similar or identical situations. Or parents living with their parents so that they could all raise the kids.

We never really went anywhere, but I had a good childhood, man. I didn't want to go anywhere. I had cousins to

hang with, you included. I kept busy, trailed Kokum wher-
ever she went. Then, when I was about eight or nine, my dad
tried to gain custody of me. It was fucked up. (A sigh, a snort.)
It was too late for that. Kokum had signed the papers back
when I was born. My dad made a big fucking deal about it.
He confronted her many times. He was desperate and Kokum
didn't understand. He didn't have anything to do with me
until then, really. But I think I get it. A child gives you purpose,
someone to care about. He was in his late twenties with little
in his life to motivate him. He was lost. My kokum wouldn't
give in to his pleas, though. I wasn't sure how to feel about it.
I didn't know him, not really. Kokum asked me one night if I
wanted to live with him and I thought about it for a few min-
utes, then said, I don't think so, and that was that. Later that
year my dad promised to take me to the rodeo, to the fair, but
he didn't show. And to stop me from crying, Kokum drove me
to town herself. She rode every ride I wanted to go on, took
a bunch of Gravol and rode the Ferris wheel with me until
midnight, when the fireworks went off. She didn't complain
at all. I still thought about him, though. I still wanted him to
be in my life more.

Something shifted inside me. I asked more questions
about both him and my mom. Kokum always tried to answer
them, but I could tell they started to worry her, she didn't
know how truthful she could be with me. It didn't make sense
to me, dude, why there weren't really answers. As a teen, I
tried to be a good kid, but it was hard. Most of my friends
were out partying and having sex and doing drugs, it was like
I didn't have a choice. I always felt alone. School became an

excuse to hang with the few friends I did have. Weekends we slept wherever we could. I remember one party where I got so drunk I blacked out and woke up in a fucking inflatable pool. (Laughter.) We did all the stupid shit you do when you're a teen bored as fuck on the rez. I was having sex by the time I was fourteen. I felt so pleased with myself back then but now I'm like, damn, maybe that was too early. STIs when you're fifteen, sixteen, not a good look. [Jack shook his head.] One summer I moved into a girl's house, I was still fifteen. I thought that was it, we were in love and I'd be with her forever. Obviously, that's not what happened. She dumped me for some white kid. I was angry as fuck. We beat the shit out of him. I'm not proud of that, don't get me wrong. He was okay, thank god. But back then I didn't care. Kokum tried to get through to me. She saw me spiral, didn't want me to fuck things up. She wanted me to graduate high school so bad. Only some of our family had. It would mean she was a good parent. I couldn't even give her that, man. Like, what the fuck? When I thought I got that one girl pregnant, I thought my life had ended, that I was going to be exactly like my parents. Kokum said she'd help raise the kid. I didn't even ask her to. She said we'd get through it together, and I believed her. I started wanting to have that kid, even if the girl and I weren't going to stay in a relationship. Then, well, you know what happened next.

After that, most days I felt like I didn't have control over my life. Fate controlled me. Even when I tried to live with you, I knew it wasn't going to work. I fucking hated that job at Walmart. They paid me nothing, barely minimum wage.

Plus, the managers were racist. Always checked my pockets to see if I'd stolen anything at the end of a shift. I was so damn homesick, man. I don't know why I couldn't talk to you about it. I didn't want to distract you. You were so concentrated on your studies. So I left. I barely even said goodbye to you. I hate that I did that. I moved back to the rez and, well, set in motion the shit that got me here. [Jack looked around the small room. He let his head drop, as if to say that the story had exhausted him. I wondered if it was a story he had told before. I allowed the quiet to envelop us.]

I thought I'd hidden everything from Kokum. I did everything at night, when she was asleep, when I thought she was asleep. I left my window open and snuck in and out of it. I drove in and out of the driveway with the headlights turned off. I didn't enter the house unless I was sober or at least barely drunk or high. I did odd jobs around the rez— a bit of carpentry, landscaping. Things felt under control. But there was no control, obviously. I understand that now. She knew everything. One night she was on the porch when I snuck out. She called out for me, so I started running, faster than I ever have. Ain't that fucked up? Like she was some wild animal, like I was being chased. I ran until I was at the train tracks that meant I was almost out of the rez. I stood on the tracks and sobbed. Screamed and screamed. It was humiliating. All I felt was regret, guilt, shame, nothing else, there wasn't room inside me to feel anything else. She was still awake when I returned that morning. She didn't say anything, just hugged me. I couldn't open my eyes, couldn't hug her back. She hugged tighter and tighter. Maybe, in a way, she was saying goodbye. I don't know. Shit got worse after that. I was careless. Stopped trying to find work, stopped sleeping, spent most of my time in my truck in the driveway. Not too long after that I got arrested. Still don't know how that cop knew I'd been drinking; I was driving perfectly, I wasn't drunk. I guess we're always breaking the law in their eyes. He made me get out of the truck, before trying to Breathalyze me or anything else, like I was going to maul him. I've never felt so scared, man. I felt like a kid, a little boy. I thought he was going to kill me, so I didn't say anything, didn't move, just laid down on the ground with my hands behind my back. The cop knelt on me; I felt winded, couldn't speak or think. I almost passed out. In the holding cells that night I swore I would change, would quit everything, didn't wanna end up in jail. I was released that morning, but only because the cop didn't follow protocol. I smartened up for a few days, really thought I could be sober, then, well, you know how it goes. When I got arrested the second time, the cops had a warrant because someone narced on me, told them I'd tried to sell to him, to his kids. She saw the arrest happen this time. We were both outside; it was such a sunny afternoon. It all happened so quickly. I looked over at her standing in the garden and felt nothing. Not sadness, not fear, not anger. For the first time in a long time, I couldn't tell what she was thinking. It fucked me up a bit, man. It was as if I'd lost her, as if we were strangers all of a sudden. I couldn't say "sorry" or anything. It didn't matter, I thought at the time. Nothing could change the fact that I was being arrested. They threw me into the jail cell. I didn't sleep at all that night. I had such intense anxiety it felt like someone was pushing on my chest. Whenever I was almost asleep that crushing feeling would come back and I'd jump up and scream. My brain thought someone was attacking me. All I could think about was how much drugs they had found and how stupid it was of me not to hide them better. I hoped Kokum wouldn't be charged at all and then I worried about what would happen if she was.

The next afternoon was my bail hearing. The judge decided that because of my prior run-ins with the cops, the evidence against me, and fear that I would continue to deal, I would await trial at the Remand in Edmonton. I'd done the drive dozens of times, but that day the four hours felt like a whole fucking lifetime. There were no windows in the back of the police van, so I couldn't even stare at the damn trees. Being inside that van was like being inside my own head. There was no difference.

I went through withdrawal when I first got here. No one gave a shit. I sweated so much my uniform, my sheets, my socks, were always drenched. I thought my lungs were going to collapse. I wanted to kill myself. I started seeing shit that wasn't there. My body ached. I couldn't sit still, couldn't walk. The guards kept telling me to calm down, to stop making a disturbance. I told them to go fuck themselves. I know I should've kept my mouth shut, but I was angry. Then came the vomiting and shitting. I didn't even know I was an addict, man. I just wanted not to be anxious, to escape. I didn't think about nothing when I was high. When I'm sober I'm always thinking about fucked-up things. That's been the worst part of this. Too much time to think, nothing but time. All of my money would go to drugs and alcohol. I had to start deal-ing to pay for more. I owe some guys thousands of dollars. They'll be waiting for me when I get out. It's a vicious cycle. I might not get out of it. I want to, though. I don't want to be here. I don't want to be in jail, don't want to end up back in here. Some guys have been trying to get me to join their crews, but I say no, say I'm not about that life. They call me a pussy, a fag . . . no offense.

Every time Kokum visits, my heart fucking breaks, man. She keeps saying, "When you get out . . ." Part of me thinks I'll be here for years. My court date keeps getting pushed back. The lawyer they gave me is shitty, doesn't give a fuck about me. I'm sure I'm just another native dude he won't mind to see behind bars even if it's his job to get me out. All of this hurts Kokum more than it does me. I can't even hug her. She can't hug me. It's all she wants, I can tell. I want to be bet-ter for her. I want her to see that her love made a difference. I don't know how I deserve her. She's been my mom and my dad. I probably took advantage of her love at times, but that's a burden I carry, that I have to repair. I need to forgive myself. I was barely an adult when I got into all this shit. Dealing was easy. I made money faster than I ever had. I didn't know what I was supposed to do with my life anyway. I lived day-to-day, man. If I started thinking bigger than that I set myself up for failure. I didn't have a future. I had a past.

To pass the time in here I've been going to the classes they offer. I even sat in on one about native history. I thought about you the whole time, thought maybe you'd walk into the pod one day to teach something, talk to us about the protests and the schools and all the theft. Why hadn't I learned about all that before? Did you? The government fucked our ancestors over, again and again. No wonder there are so many of us in here. Fuck, there are about a dozen from our rez, the nearby reserves. Most are here on similar drug charges. Some for weed, which is fucked up, since it's legal now. Like me, most of them don't have a court date. One of them just got out yesterday and we all said a prayer for him. I don't talk to anyone about home, though, I can't bring myself to. Whenever someone does, I walk up and leave. In the native class, the teacher mentioned our rez, said we might read a poem written by someone from there, and I almost teared up, man. I couldn't believe it. I was so happy. I'm so emotional in here nowadays, it's confusing. And lonely. [Laughter.]

All I'm good for is love, I think. I really do want a wife and a kid, a Jack Junior. I want a little house on the rez, next to Kokum's maybe, if Chief and Council will give me one, but who knows, since none of our relatives are elected. [Laughter.] I want Mary to be a chapan, to get another shot. I want someone else to be loved by her, to experience that blessing. She even tried to lie to the police for me, would tell them I wasn't home when I was half-awake in the bedroom steps away. I hate that I put her in that position. She really did try to give me a good life, man.

I want a family, is what I'm saying. But I can't do that until I know I won't leave them. I don't want anyone to go through what I went through. I was abandoned. No kid understands that decision. I blamed myself, thought there was something wrong with me. I couldn't shake that feeling,

*no matter how much Kokum tried to love it out of me. I keep
waiting for them to apologize. Fuck, I've even hoped that I'd
see them in your seat one of these Saturdays, that my mom
or my dad would see me in this fucking outfit and feel bad
or guilty or at least sad. I've gotta let that go, though, man.
It's eating me alive. It has been for a long time now. I need to
unlearn so much. "Unlearn" is one of the words the teacher
taught us, by the way. See, I'm learning, man. I realize that
was all messed up. I want to do things differently. I want to
take care of someone, protect them. The first thing I'm going
to do when I get out is download Tinder. [Laughter.] Well,
that and maybe rehab, but I already feel different. I know I'm
going to change my life.*

*I want to be a good man, a good dad. That's it. I don't
need anything else, anything more. Being neglected, not being
raised by my parents, I'm no psychologist but I think that's
how this all began. That history, and the history of the country too. My fate was determined from the start. The drugs,
the dealing, the alcohol, they let me be more than what I was.
They freed me from myself. That make sense? But I can be
more than that. I can escape that cycle. Write that in your
book. [Laughter.] This book, I can't wait to read it. To be
honest, when I first heard about the book I was angry. I wondered: How are our lives so different? We used to hang as
kids, but now we're nothing alike. I'm in here and you're out
there. That's the main difference, really, that massive difference. But, at the end of the day, I'm so proud of you, man.
Why haven't I told you that before? You seem happy, dude.
Are you happy?*

A guard entered, instructed us that a visitor for another inmate had arrived. There wasn't time to say goodbye; Jack was already being escorted back to his pod.

•

Was I happy? That evening I sat down at my desk to finally begin writing the novel I hoped would answer the question.

ACKNOWLEDGMENTS

Works cited: Roland Barthes's *Mourning Diary*, James Baldwin's *Giovanni's Room*, Mary Oliver's poem "The Summer Day," Judith Butler's *Senses of the Subject*, Carl Phillips's *Reconnaissance*, Yiyun Li's *Where Reasons End*, Ocean Vuong's *On Earth We're Briefly Gorgeous*, Audre Lorde's poem "A Litany for Survival," Fred Moten and Stefano Harney's *The Undercommons*, Clarice Lispector's *Água Viva*, Kogonada's film *Columbus*, Maggie Nelson's *On Freedom*.

The first line of the first chapter nods to the first line of Brandon Taylor's *Real Life*.

The protagonist's thoughts on cliché are in conversation

with the line "What if life could be saved by clichés?" in Yiyun Li's *Where Reasons End*.

The phrase ". . . to stand in the middle of paradox like a doorway and not budge" is in conversation with Dionne Brand's *A Map to the Door of No Return*.

•

Thank you to my astute and lovely editors David and Mo. I'm a better writer because of their company.

Thank you to my agent Stephanie, who was this book's first reader and fiercest champion. Thank you as well to her colleagues at CookeMcDermid.

Hazlitt published an early draft of the chapter "People Were Crying." Haley Cullingham's feedback was invaluable.

Shout-out to the cafés in Edmonton, Treaty 6 territory, where I wrote much of the first draft: Second Cup in South Common and Square 1 Coffee. I wrote subsequent drafts in Vancouver on the unceded and ancestral lands of the Musqueam, Squamish, and Tsleil-Waututh.

Thank you to family and friends—my saviors, my heroes.